Double Trouble Path

Path Series Wedding Novella

by:

Neri Lopez

Double Trouble Path

The Path Series: Book 4.5 A Wedding Novella

Neri Lopez

Siren Book & Craft LLC

Reader Discretion

This work includes themes of sexual assault and rape that some readers may find disturbing or triggering. Reader discretion is advised.

If you or someone you know has been sexually assaulted, please know that you are not alone and that there are resources that can help you through this difficult time. If you are or have been a victim of sexual assault, you can contact your local police department as well as call the number below.

National Sexual Assault Hotline:
800-656-4673
Or chat online at: http://www.rainn.org

RAINN (Rape, Abuse & Incest National Network) is the nation's largest anti-sexual violence organization. RAINN created and operated the National Sexual Assault Hotline in partnership with over 1,000 sexual assault service providers across the country.
For victims of a roofie assault, please contact:
844-960-2939
http://www.theedgetreatment.com

Also, help is available 24/7 on the **Suicide and Crisis Lifeline**. You can call or text in English or Spanish.
The number is: **988**
http://988lifeline.org

Rock 'n' Roll Resort & Casino

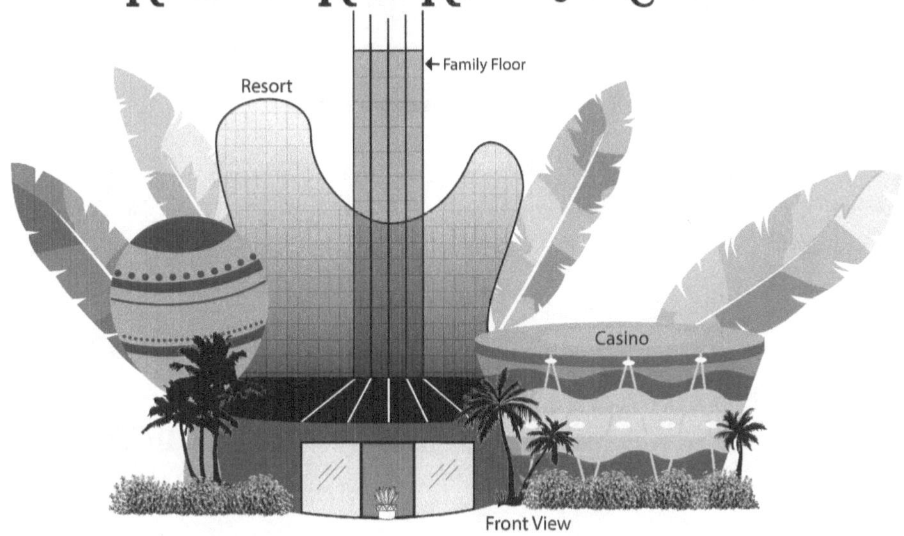

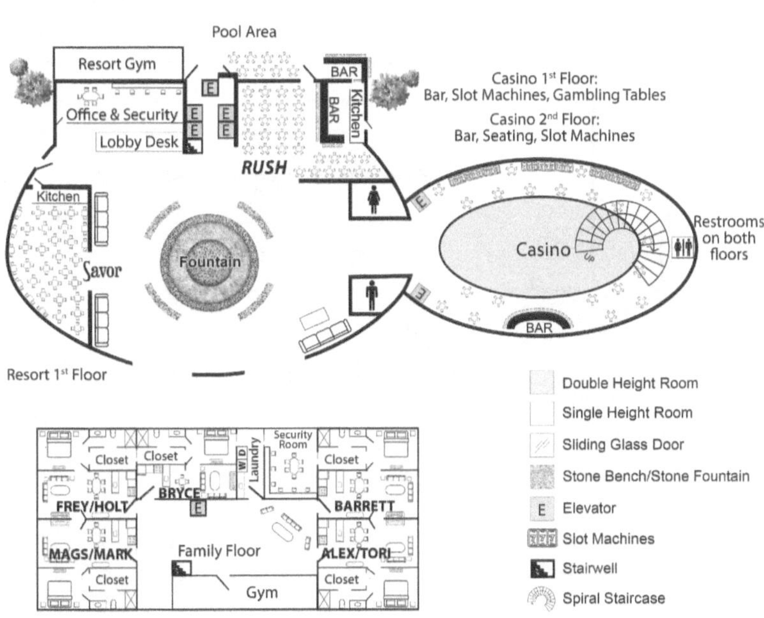

Rock 'n' Roll Resort & Casino

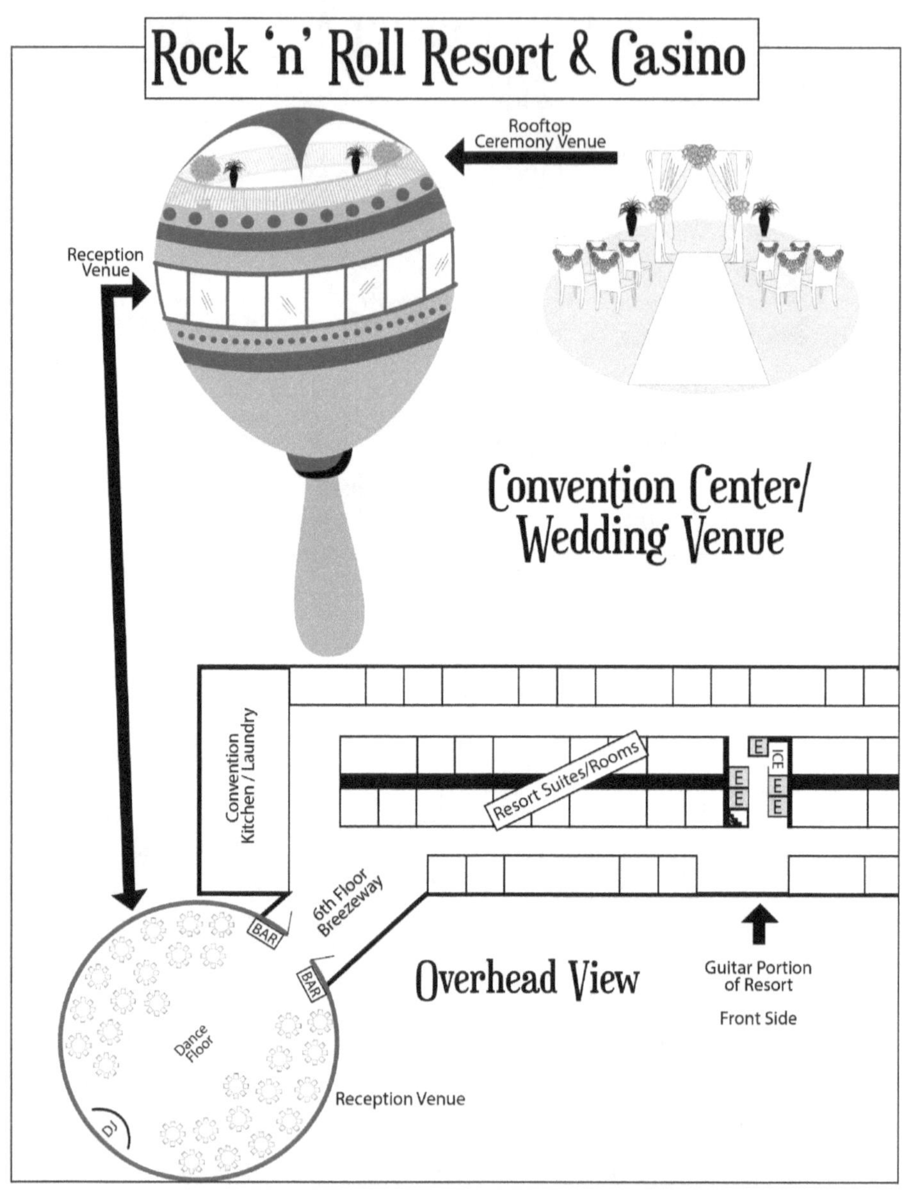

Path Series Family Trees

*d.-deceased * div.-divorced * a.-adopted * shaded box is a spouse*

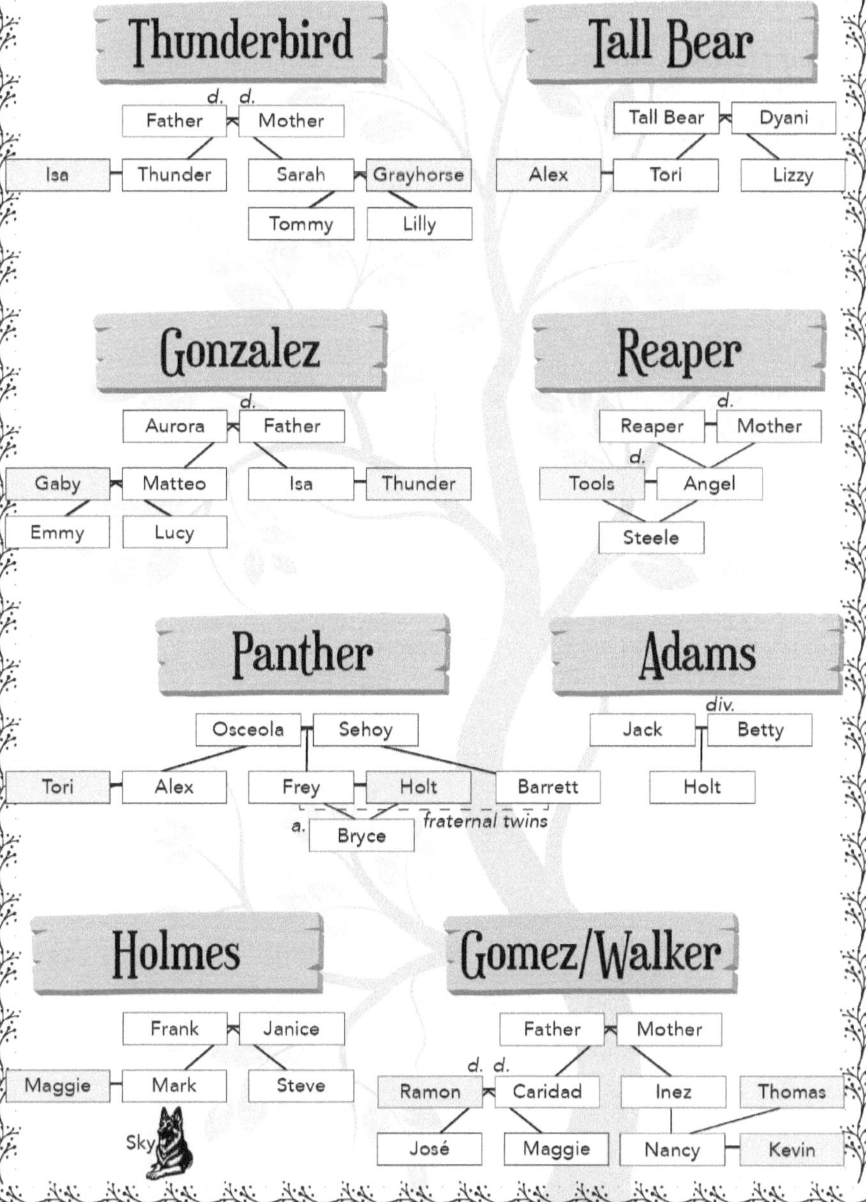

Lakota Translations
Até – father
Cuŋwítku- daughter (her)
Iná – mother
Lekší – uncle
Pilámaya – thank you
Tibló – brother
Wakan Tanka – Great Spirit

Seminole Translations
Chakpootsi – son
Chackshosti – daughter
Chatski – mother

Spanish Translations
Abuela – grandmother
Ay, Dios mío – oh my God
Cómo estás – how are you
Dale, mi niña – let's go, my girl
El Loco – the crazy one (aka José)
Hermanita – little sister
Qué guapos – how handsome
Qué paso – what happened

Contents

Chapter 1

Dress Pickup Day

FREY

"Aahh!" Frey screamed and stormed into Tori's room after Alex opened the door. Grabbing Tori's hands, she jumped up and down, pulling Tori along for the ride. Today was their last fitting at the bridal store on Las Olas Blvd. If everything fit perfectly, Frey and Tori were bringing their dresses home. Sehoy (Frey's mom), Dyani (Tori's mom), Maggie (their friend), and Lizzy (Tori's little sister) were going with them to get their first look. Alex and Holt wanted to accompany them and protect them from any trouble, but Frey banned them. She wanted to keep the dresses hidden to respect the tradition of the groom not seeing the bridal gown before the wedding. But after lots of disagreements over their safety, Frey agreed to allow Mark (Maggie's boyfriend) and Barrett (Frey's twin brother) to be their security.

Everyone was on alert because of the attacks that were still going on between the two rival motorcycle clubs Lucifer's Renegades (LRs) and Los Lobos de Muerte which was why Maggie and Tori were not supposed to leave the family floor at the Rock 'n' Roll Resort & Casino. The LRs attempted to kidnap Tori, a month before they kidnapped Maggie because of her brother, José, who was the sergeant-at-arms for Los Lobos.

"I can't wait to see our finished dresses!" Tori exclaimed while jumping.

"Ladies." Alex stood behind Tori with his fingers in his ears. "Can you keep the screaming down?"

"Nice try, bro." Holt was behind Frey with his arms crossed and a shit-eating grin on his face.

Frey stopped jumping and slapped Alex's shoulder. "Don't ruin our day, grumpy."

"I'm not grumpy." Alex shrugged. "I just don't want you to wake up the whole damn floor."

"Why not? All the ladies and some guys are going with us today." Frey poked Alex in the chest. "Besides, it's almost time to go."

"I don't know why we can't come." Alex rolled his eyes and crossed his arms, pouting like a two-year-old who wanted his way.

Frey watched, anticipating a floor-pounding tantrum.

"We could just stay in the car." Alex pleaded with his eyes at Frey and Tori.

"Nope." Tori walked to him and hugged him. "We'll be back soon. I love you."

"Love you too," Alex humphed before he kissed her.

Frey turned to face Holt, who was laughing at Alex's antics. She was relieved Holt was behaving appropriately as her fiancé and not interfering with their plans.

"Come on, Holtie." Frey grabbed his hand and pulled him toward Barrett's room. "Time to get everyone together so we can leave."

"You got it, darlin'." Holt followed Frey.

The girls devised a plan for gathering everyone. Frey got Barrett from his room while Tori got her mom and sister. Dyani and Lizzy were staying in Bryce's (the shelter boy Frey and Holt are adopting) future room for the weekend. Then Frey got Mark and Maggie. They all gathered in front of the elevator, heading down to meet Sehoy in the resort lobby.

"*Chackshosti*." Sehoy greeted Frey and Tori when they stepped off the elevator. Sehoy began calling Tori 'daughter' in her native Seminole language as soon as Tori said yes to Alex's proposal. "Are you girls ready?"

"I'm so excited, *chatski*." Frey hugged her mom.

"Yes." Tori hugged Sehoy. "I can't wait for you to see our dresses."

"Stay here." Barrett interrupted them. "I'll bring the resort van around."

With eight people going on a small adventure, Frey asked to borrow the van. Of course, her parents had agreed. Being a security officer, Barrett was used to driving the van, making him the designated driver. Pulling up to the resort, Barrett let everyone into the van. Barrett and Mark were in the front seat while Sky, his K-9 police dog, got many belly rubs in the back. Sky was a hit with all the ladies, who happily welcomed her into their Bride Tribe.

At the bridal shop, Frey checked them in and requested the shop's larger fitting room so everyone could fit. Frey forbid the guys from entering the shop because she didn't want either of them to peek and share what they saw with Alex or Holt. Mark and Barrett agreed to it, as long as Sky stood watch at their fitting room door. The boys kept telling them they didn't want to take any chances.

With a dramatic flourish all her own, Frey was the first to dress and open the curtain. She had chosen a low plunging A-line dress with tulle for the skirt. The back of the sleeveless bodice featured two beaded strands crossing from shoulder to shoulder, adorned with a small bow where the bodice met the skirt. Both brides were going to wear these wedding dresses for the ceremony, but then changing into their American Indian wedding outfits their mothers made for their reception. Frey chose not to wear a veil.

"Oh, *chackshosti*." Sehoy covered her mouth, tears welling up in her eyes. "It looks perfect on you."

Smiling, Frey grabbed the sides of her dress and spun around in front of the mirror. Everyone was commenting on how gorgeous she looked. She couldn't believe she was finally marrying her childhood crush and the love of her life. After overcoming several obstacles, they were finally going to be together and adopt Bryce. She couldn't wait to start her life as a wife to Holt and stepmom to Bryce.

The store seamstress walked into the room, smiling at Frey. "How does it feel?"

"It feels perfect." Frey spun again. "I love it!"

The seamstress walked around Frey, checking it out. "It looks perfect."

"Thank you." Frey beamed at her.

"Frey." Tori grabbed her hands. "You look beautiful. Holt will be beside himself when he sees you."

"Thank you, bestie." Frey hugged her. "Now, help me take this off so we can see yours."

Frey pulled the curtain closed and Tori unzipped Freya's dress. The seamstress placed the dress inside a white garment bag carefully, making sure not to wrinkle it.

"Frey." Tori faced her. "Can you stay in here and help me get dressed?"

"Absolutely." Frey unzipped Tori's garment bag with her dress inside. While some brides seek to make their weddings all about themselves, Frey was happy to share it with her closest friend. The day Tori moved into their hotel while she worked at the American Indian Cultural Center had been the best day of her life. Who knew that day would mark the beginning of a friendship that was more like a sisterhood. The idea of her best friend marrying her brother Alex had never occurred to her, but now that it was happening, she was ecstatic.

She hoped her twin Barrett would someday pick a girl who would be another sister to her. She doubted if it would ever happen, since Barrett seemed to be a perpetual bachelor.

*** Tori ***

Tori had dreamed about this day since she was a little girl. She often dreamed about what she would wear, who she would marry, and what he would look like. She always thought it would be someone from her reservation, not realizing at such a young age that she would meet the man of her dreams so far away. Although Alex wasn't from her tribe, Oglala Lakota, she loved he was an American Indian. They were from different tribes, but they shared the same values and hopes for their future. They both agreed to teach their children both languages and cultures. It was important for future generations to learn about their ancestor's history—the good and the bad.

Alex was her perfect other half. He'd been so patient in helping her get therapy and overcome the horrible things Winston had done to her. To this day, she still didn't remember the details of the rape, and she'd stopped trying. She wanted to be a survivor, not a victim. Dwelling on the past would not help her move forward with her life.

"Hey, turn that frown upside down." Frey held up her dress and grabbed her shoulder. "Today, you only need to think about good things. No sad thoughts."

"You're right." Tori smiled at her as she carefully pulled on her dress. "Can you help me with the veil?"

Tori's bun helped Frey easily slide the comb with the veil attached. Tori turned around and smiled at Frey. "How do I look?"

"Stunning. My brother is a very lucky man."

"Thank you." Tori's eyes glistened with unshed tears. "We will soon be sisters."

"Yep." Frey reached out and squeezed Tori's hands. "I feel honored to call you my sister."

A tear slipped down Tori's face. They were tears of joy and acceptance. The Panther family had accepted her with all the love they had to give. Since her family lived in South Dakota, having a loving family here meant everything to her.

"No crying." Frey wiped her tear. "Let's go out there and wow everyone with your beauty."

"Okay." Tori grinned.

Frey grabbed the end of the curtain and pushed it open, standing aside so everyone could see Tori. Tori's dress was an off the shoulder lacey bodice with long lacey sleeves. Where Frey's skirt was all tulle, Tori's was satin with lacey appliques all the way to the bottom. Her veil was a cathedral length with the same lacey appliques around the border.

"*Cuŋwítku,* you look beautiful." Dyani grabbed Lizzy's hand and shed tears of joy.

"*Pilámaya, iná.*" Tori thought she'd pulled herself together after Frey's comment until she saw her mom's joyful tears streaming down her face. Then all bets were off, and she lost it. Dyani got up to give her a hug.

"Wow." Lizzy stood and walked toward Tori. "You look beautiful, sis."

"Shit, you both are going to be the most beautiful brides ever." Maggie blurted.

Frey pointed at Maggie. "You, young lady, are very lucky Lucy (Gaby's daughter, resident potty mouth police, and creative hairstylist) isn't here to hear you cuss."

"You're right." Maggie rolled her eyes. "At the rate Mark and I are going, we'll be paying for her college education instead of her parents. She might need a new swear jar soon."

They all laughed while Tori told the seamstress it was also perfect and changed back into her clothes. As they stepped out of the fitting room, Tori noticed Barrett and Mark standing with their arms crossed in the lobby instead of outside.

"Hey," Frey screamed at Barrett while she barreled toward him, slugging him on the shoulder. "What are you doing in here? Did you peek?"

"Absolutely not." Barrett held up his hands in surrender. "We came in because people were looking at us funny. Being in here was less conspicuous."

"He's right." Mark pointed at Barrett. "I promise we didn't look."

"Are we all set?" Barrett asked when the seamstress brought their dresses to the register.

"We are." Frey and Tori both took out their wallets to make their final dress payment.

"I got this." Sehoy made her way to the counter.

"No, Sehoy, you don't need to do this." Tori attempted to stop her.

"This is part of my gift to you both. It's not every day your daughter gets married, and you gain another daughter. Tori, I already argued with your parents, and they agreed to let me do this for you." Sehoy looked at Dyani. Tori turned to face her mom and saw her nod her head.

"Okay." Tori hugged Sehoy. "Thank you."

"Thank you, *chatski*." Frey gave her mom a kiss on the cheek.

"You're welcome, ladies. Now, let's get these dresses back to the resort so we can eat lunch at Savor." Sehoy waved to Barrett, who came over, grabbed their dresses, and carried them to the car. "Alex said he would make something nice for us."

"Don't you dare unzip those bags!" Frey yelled at Barrett.

"Yeah, yeah, yeah." Barrett said, on his way out.

Chapter 2

What the Hell?

ANGEL

Although Angel despised entering the clubhouse, she needed to speak with Numbers, Reaper's closest friend and the MC's accountant. Her hatred for Los Lobos risked the lives of her son, Steele, and herself. She struggled to prevent Steele from going to the clubhouse. His fascination with Lucifer's Renegades MC (the LRs) stemmed from his father (Tools) being a member and his grandfather (Reaper) being the president. While Tools was alive, Angel allowed Steele to work with his father at the garage he ran for the LRs. Tools built the garage to help the LRs go legit. Unfortunately, that became a lost cause after his passing.

The LRs now employed in the garage behaved rudely and made threats to customers. If Tools were still alive, he would never have tolerated that behavior. Angel now recognized the LRs would never become legitimate. They would always be a one-percenter club with her asshole father, Reaper, as their leader. But these rival wars with the Los Lobos MC were the worst. They had to end.

A few days ago, when she got home from work to an empty house, she figured Steele was still at a friend's place studying. Numbers shocked her when he dropped Steele off, explaining their lateness was because of a fire at the clubhouse. Numbers explained how he rescued Steele, getting him to safety before the fire spread. She was grateful to Numbers for saving her son, but angry that Steele had lied and called Numbers to take him to the clubhouse. With Reaper now in jail, she had forbidden Steele from going to the clubhouse, but obviously he wasn't listening, and Numbers wasn't helping.

Numbers and her father were childhood friends. Angel underestimated Steele's closeness to Numbers. She thought her biggest threat was sitting in a jail cell only to find out – she had another threat closer to home. Numbers not only continued to insert himself into Steele's life, but he also persistently hit on her, making it increasingly difficult to evade his advances.

Angel decided to confront Numbers today and tell him to leave her son alone. Following the Los Lobos fire that damaged their clubhouse, the LRs moved their meetings to the back office at the garage. The prospective gang members (the prospects) hanging out in the waiting area disregarded her when she walked past them because she was Reaper's daughter.

Holding her head high, she followed the sound of Numbers' raised voice to the back office. He was yelling at someone about fucking up a wedding. *Fuck up what wedding?* Angel thought. *Who was getting married?* Not believing it to be one of their private 'church' meetings since the door was wide open, she strolled into the room with as much confidence as she could muster. Stopping dead in her tracks, she looked around the room as all the brothers turned to stare at her. *Shit, they were having a club meeting. Why was the door open? Why hadn't any of the prospects stopped her? What the hell was going on?* Club meetings were considered important and private by the LRs, so the door was never left open. She walked into the viper's nest.

"Angel, what are you doing here?" Numbers put his arm around Steele, who sat next to him at the head of the table.

"Uh, um, I was looking for Steele." Why was her son sitting so comfortably next to Numbers, holding the gavel? "He needs to come home."

"I'll bring him home when we finish. Right, son?" Numbers patted Steele's back to get his attention.

"Yes, sir."

What the fuck was happening? And since when did Numbers call Steele son. She had to get Steele away from him. She didn't want Steele to join the LRs.

"Are you now president?" Angel looked around the room, gaging everyone's expressions.

"I'm interim president until your father gets out." Numbers sat up and squared his shoulders.

This was not good. If Numbers called the shots, he could easily decide to promote Steele to a prospect and move him up the ranks quicker. Club members didn't argue with their president. It didn't matter that he was a temporary president.

"You look busy. I can take him now." Angel walked toward Steele and grabbed his hand. "Let's go home." Steele continued to stare at the table and pulled his hand out of her grasp.

Numbers laughed along with some brothers. "It looks like he wants to stay here with us. I'll drive him home when we finish. Go home Angel. I'll talk to you later."

Who the hell did he think he was? "You are not his father, Numbers. I'm taking him home now." Angel grabbed Steele's bicep and pulled him up out of the chair. She saw Numbers' red, angry face before he bolted up from his chair, hand flying out to slap her face before she had time to back away. *Fuck, that hurt!*

"Don't you ever talk back to me." Numbers growled and grabbed Steele's other bicep, pulling him out of her grasp. "Now get the fuck out and go home. He's where he needs to be."

Placing a hand on her burning cheek, Angel winced. Numbers had never hit her before. Shocked, she decided it was safest to leave the room before his anger turned toward Steele because of her disobedience. "Yeah, okay."

Leaving the room, Angel stood outside, silently trying to eavesdrop on their plans.

"Do you want me to make sure she left?" Brick, the LRs new Enforcer since Bull was arrested along with Reaper, asked.

"No," Numbers answered. "She knows better. Steele, have a seat son, so we can continue."

"Where is this wedding?" A brother asked.

"At that maraca looking thing, they just added to the Rock 'n' Roll Resort & Casino." Numbers grunted.

"Anyone in particular we should look for at this wedding?" Another brother asked.

"Who the fuck do you think, asshole!" Numbers shouted.

The room became so silent Angel could hear a pin. Then Numbers continued with his rant.

"If you see José or his bitch of a sister, Maggie, kill them. Also, that little prissy bitch Tori that got Reaper put in jail. With her gone, maybe he stands a chance of getting off since she can't testify at his trial if she's dead."

Angel knew her father's club killed people, but to hear the words so callously spoken made her sick, especially since her son was sitting in a room full of murderers. *Would they turn Steele into a murderer too?* She had to get Steele away from them.

"When is this fucking shitshow wedding?" Brick asked.

Angel leaned in closer to hear the details.

"On Sunday, New Year's Eve." Numbers announced.

"That's in two fucking days?"

"You don't think I know that!" Numbers screamed and slammed his hand on the table. "We need to get our shit together and set up a plan. Reaper wants everyone there. We're gonna fucking spray the place with bullets. Snake, you were a sniper. I need you to target those two bitches." Numbers yelled.

Oh Shit. Angel covered her mouth and slowly tiptoed backwards out of the hallway. Acting like nothing happened, she waved to the prospects and got in her car. It was Friday night, and they were going to kill Tori and Maggie on Sunday, New Year's Eve. She had to warn them and keep Steele away from them. But how was she going to do that since the American Indian Cultural Center was closed this week and she didn't know where Maggie lived?

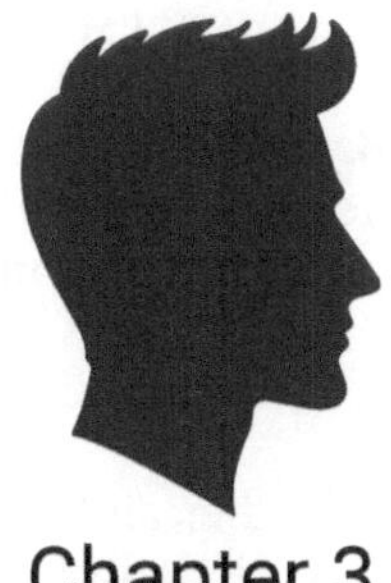

Chapter 3

Distract our Women

Holt

Holt was aware Frey would organize a Bachelorette Party for the girls following the Bridal Shower on Saturday, the evening prior to the wedding. He preferred his fiancée not be hungover at their wedding. This morning, he wanted to share his plan with the boys.

While the girls ate lunch at Savor following their dress pickup, he texted them to meet in his room. After everyone arrived, he called Matteo and put him on speakerphone.

"Okay." Holt placed his phone on the cocktail table in his living room and faced them. "Now that we're all here, let's get started. I have a great idea for stopping the girls from going out after the bridal shower without us."

"What the hell are you talking about?" Barrett asked.

"You know, between Frey and Maggie, they will get the girls to go out and get drunk the night before the wedding." Holt crossed his arms, facing all the guys sitting on the couch watching him.

"True." Mark shook his head. "Maggie's all about celebrating."

"So." Alex looked at Holt. "What's your plan, oh great one?"

"I think we need to strip for them." Holt blurted, knowing he was going to get some flak for what he just said.

"What?" Thunder looked confused.

"What the fuck did you just say?" Alex sat forward, planting his elbows on his knees.

"I'm not stripping for anyone but my wife." Grayhorse snorted.

"Have you lost your fucking mind?" Mark looked at him like he was a lunatic.

Alex stood up and walked to Holt.

Holt expected Alex to support him, but Alex unexpectedly struck him in the back of the head like when they were kids. "What the hell was that for?" Holt stepped away from Alex rubbing his head.

"I was hoping to knock some sense into you." Alex braced his fists on his hips while the rest of them complained about Holt's plan.

"Okay. Okay." Holt raised his arms, attempting to stop them from talking. "Just listen to me. We can do a strip tease like Chippendale dancers in front of each of our women. Obviously, we are not stripping all the way. No one sees my cock but my future wife."

"Isn't it a little late for that?" Barrett coughed into his fist.

"Not funny, motherfucker!" Holt pointed at Barrett. "You wait until you fall for the love of your life and she finds out how many women have seen your cock."

"Children." Thunder grumbled. "Keep talking, Holt. Why do you think this would work?"

"If we sidetrack them with our bodies and sexy dance skills, they'll want to stay with us and not go out." Holt smiled, proud of himself for coming up with such a brilliant plan.

"Mark and Matteo are the only ones with sexy dance skills." Alex grumbled.

"You're just saying that because Mark's taken a shit ton of dance lessons growing up and, well, Matteo is Hispanic and moves his hips like a pro." Holt shrugged.

"That's a compliment, right?" Matteo's voice came from the phone.

"I am not stripping." Barrett bolted off the couch. "I don't have a woman in the mix. I'll be the emcee. You love struck assholes can dance."

"I'm in." Mark smiled.

"Of course you are." Alex kicked his ankle.

"Hey, I can teach you some moves." Mark pumped his hips and moved his arms while he was sitting on the couch.

"Hey." Barrett snapped his fingers. "You guys can be like the village people. You each wear a costume. Who's gonna be the cowboy?" Barrett wiggled his eyebrows.

"That's easy." Thunder pointed with his thumb at Grayhorse. "He's got chaps."

"Fine." Grayhorse grunted. "But if I'm the cowboy, you're the Indian."

"Done." Thunder shrugged. "Isa loves my pow-wow regalia without the speedo."

"Can we please not talk about what my sister likes?" Matteo grumbled.

"You better keep your junk in your loincloth, or Sarah will freak out." Grayhorse glared at him. "A sister shouldn't see her brother's cock naked, swinging around."

"Stop, please!" Matteo screamed.

"Noted." Thunder nodded.

"I'll be a businessman." Matteo sighed. "I got lots of suits."

"That's great. Alex, you can be a chef with your apron." Barrett pointed at Alex. "But wear pants underneath or Frey will have a cow." Then he looked at Mark and Holt. "Who wants to be the cop or the construction worker?"

"I'll be the construction worker." Mark raised his arm. "I'm very familiar with that type of work growing up on a ranch."

"That leaves you as the cop." Barrett pointed at Holt.

"Fine, I'll be the cop. Women love a guy in uniform." Holt smiled. "Let's pick a song. We'll have to practice our moves when the girls aren't around, and we can do a few runs during the bridal shower. It's best to keep this as a surprise."

"Wait, aren't Emmy and Lucy going to be there for the shower?" Thunder leaned forward, forearms resting on his knees.

"We can ask my mom to take the girls." Matteo volunteered Aurora.

"We'll also get my mom and Tori's mom to go with them. I really don't want to do this in front of my mom." Alex smirked at Holt.

"Okay. We'll get Sehoy, Dyani, Aurora, and Minnie to take the kids down to swim in the pool and then they can have a sleepover so we can seal the deal with our girls." Holt nodded.

"Who's going to take the kids for the sleepover if you all are trying to 'seal the deal'?" Barrett did air quotes.

"I can talk to Minnie and Skip." Grayhorse suggested. "They've all been there before. Or Sarah and I can take them to our house. We've sealed the deal many times with our kids in the house."

"Of course you have," Thunder muttered and elbowed Grayhorse in the stomach.

"Okay. Where should we meet during the bridal shower?" Holt looked at everyone.

"I'll find an available suite near this floor and text everyone." Barrett threw his arm over Holt's shoulder. "Good job, bro. This is awesome! I love this plan."

"Of course you do." Alex stared at Barrett. "You don't have to dance. You better not fucking videotape us."

"Moi?" Barrett placed his hand over his heart. "I would never do that."

"Fucker." Alex mumbled.

The boys made their plans and left the room before the girls finished their lunch and came looking for them.

Chapter 4

Morning of the Bridal Shower

TORI

"**G**ood morning, baby," Alex whispered in Tori's ear. "I need to run down and get the food ready for your bridal shower. Please don't go outside our door until eleven, so the ladies can finish decorating for you and Frey."

"I won't, I promise." Tori rolled over to face Alex, pulling him back into bed. "What time is it now?"

"Nine." Alex wrapped his arms around her, giving her a proper good morning kiss.

Tori couldn't be happier. She was on cloud nine. Marrying Alex was the best thing that ever happened to her. He was the love of her life. Alex made her feel special and loved. Their kiss turned hungrier. Tori tried to reach into his pants, but Alex grabbed her hand. He released her mouth, kissed her hand, and laid it over his heart.

"I love you so much." Alex gazed into her eyes. "You mean everything to me, and I can't wait to call you–my wife. Enjoy your last day as a single woman because tomorrow...you belong to me." Alex wiggled his eyebrows.

"I love you too." Tori raised her hips up against him. "Can't you stay a few more minutes?"

"No, you little minx." Alex chuckled. "I'll make it up to you tonight."

"Okay." Tori sighed.

"If you get done early, call Frey. I'm sure you can hang with her until it's time for you both to step outside your rooms." Alex got off the bed. "I'll see you later."

"Okay." Tori murmured and rolled over. She could sleep for at least another hour. Her friends and family were going to decorate the lobby of their family floor. Because her and Maggie were in hiding, a restaurant was out of the question. Tori was okay with that. They held a lot of their parties in the lobby between their rooms so they could drink and stumble to bed. The drinking part would change once Bryce moved in with Frey and Holt, but the family parties would continue. She thought about calling Frey, but she was probably getting it on with Holt. He didn't have to go to work and prepare food for their party. Lucky girl.

*** Frey ***

Frey couldn't believe she would be Mrs. Panther after tomorrow night. Holt had not only asked her dad for her hand in marriage, but he also his last name. After his mom, Betty, attacked Frey, Holt didn't want any association with his birth parents. He was ready to change his last name from Adams to Panther. Realistically, he'd been a Panther since he was in elementary school and her parents helped raise him.

"Penny for your thoughts." Holt mumbled in her neck.

He had been the big spoon last night while they slept. It was his usual position. He always said he wanted to hold her and keep her close so he could protect her. Frey didn't mind his protective side. She loved being tucked into his body at night.

"Just thinking about how happy I am to be marrying you tomorrow night." Frey scooted back, wiggling her butt into his erection, which was growing by the minute.

"I've loved you for so long." Holt pulled her closer into his body, one hand on her breast while the other slid down to her pussy. "Being with you feels like a dream. I don't want to wake up. I can't wait for us to become a family, adopt Bryce, and grow old together."

Frey was ready for this new chapter of their lives. After losing their baby, her focus was on loving Holt and officially adopting Bryce. They had already cleaned up Holt's old room and turned it into Bryce's room. Unfortunately, he couldn't move in until after the wedding. The courts liked for a couple to be married.

"Shit. You are so ready for me." Holt slid into her from behind.

His left hand on her breast tweaked and pulled her nipple while his other hand played with her clit. His body knew how to make her lose her mind. Every time with him got better and better. His hard cock pumped into her as he held her in place, driving her crazy until she came with such force it was a good thing she was lying in bed, or she would've fallen to the ground on jelly legs.

Holt never stopped pumping into her, but Frey wanted to look into his eyes when he came. She grabbed his wrists and pulled them off her body–Holt froze.

"What's wrong?" Holt groaned.

"I want to see you when you come." Frey rolled over and climbed on top of Holt. Straddling him, she rammed herself onto him.

"Fuck, sweetheart. You feel so good." Holt reached up, his hands grabbing and massaging her breasts. "I want you to come like this. I want your hot come to run down my cock and mark me as yours."

Frey loved his dirty talk. It always got her body all revved up. After her orgasm, Frey leaned down to kiss him. Holt grabbed her hips, holding her in place while he pistoned his cock into her over and over until she felt another orgasm chasing the last one.

"Shit, Holt!" Frey sat up, throwing her head back. She grabbed his biceps and ground her pussy onto him.

"Sweetheart, look at me," Holt growled. "Let me give you what you want."

Frey opened her eyes and gaped at Holt. His eyes, dilated with love and lust for her, were fixed on her.

"I love you." Frey murmured before she came again.

"I love you more." Holt grunted as he climaxed into her.

Frey collapsed onto him. Holt held her tight until their breathing slowed down to normal. He always amazed her in bed. Just when she thought she was done, he knew how to make her body do whatever he wanted.

"Shower?" Holt rolled her onto her back.

"What time is it?" Frey ran her fingers through his hair.

Holt looked at his phone, propped up on the nightstand. "Almost ten." Holt leaned down for another kiss. "When do you have to go out there?"

"Eleven." Frey mumbled against his lips.

"Good, we have time for a shower." Holt winked at her. "I'll get the water warmed up for you."

"You are the best." Frey smiled and stretched when he got off the bed.

Frey could hear the shower running and was about to get out of bed when her phone dinged with new text messages from Tori.

Tori: Hey, are you up?

Frey: Yep, getting ready to jump in the shower.

Tori: Call me when you're done. Alex left a couple hours ago to cook our food and I'm going stir crazy.

Frey: You got it.

Frey pulled the shower curtain aside and watched the water run down Holt's body while he shampooed his hair.

"What took you so long?" Holt asked while he rinsed.

"Tori texted." Frey stepped into the shower and ran her hands down Holt's chest. "She's bored and wants to come over."

Holt grunted when she wrapped her hand around his cock. "Where's Alex?"

"He went to make our food for the bridal shower." Frey dropped to her knees. "Aren't you glad you're not a chef having to cook our meal right now?" Frey grabbed his ass and shoved his cock into her mouth.

"Jesus, fuck!" Holt reached out with one hand, bracing himself on the tile wall.

Frey enjoyed surprising him and taking control. They both loved when she worshiped his cock. Although, truth be told, she loved when he ate her out too, but there was no time for that this morning. Frey took his cock to the back of her throat and swallowed twice, increasing the tightness around him. Holt held the back of her head and released his orgasm into her mouth. Frey swallowed most of it until he pulled her up, wrapped his arms around her, and dropped his cheek onto the top of her head.

"Thank you." Holt ran his fingers through her hair, holding her tightly against his chest.

Frey could hear his strong heartbeat and feel his deep breaths while he held her. "My pleasure." Frey nipped his chest.

"Sassy." Holt chuckled and slapped her ass. Grabbing her hair, he pulled her head back and kissed her.

Just as their kiss got heated, Frey pulled back. "I gotta wash up and call Tori."

"Okay. Turn around and let me wash your hair. Then I'll get out. If I wash your body, you won't see Tori, and you'll miss your bridal shower." Holt smiled and turned her to face the spigot.

Frey obliged because when he washed her hair, he also massaged her scalp. He could be her sexy hair washer any day. The only thing better than this was to lie down while he did it. His massages were so relaxing, she swayed.

"You okay, sweetheart?" Holt snickered and grabbed her around the waist, steadying her.

Frey sighed and leaned back against him, laying the back of her head on his chest.

Holt kissed the crown of her head. "Rinse. I'm gonna step out."

"Okay." Frey stepped out of his embrace and turned around.

Holt cupped her face and kissed her. "I love you. Have fun today."

"I love you, too." Frey smiled. Dropping her gaze to his ass as he stepped out of the shower. He had a really, nice ass. So round and firm. *Snap out of it.* Frey shook her head to get rid of her wayward thoughts. She had to finish up and call Tori. They had a bridal shower to attend.

Chapter 5

Bridal Shower

TORI

Tori was bouncing off the walls by the time Frey texted her. She ran through Barrett's room, the upstairs security room, laundry room, and Holt's old room to get to Frey. Thank goodness Barrett wasn't in his room. She didn't want to wake him up if he was asleep from working a late shift.

"Hey, what took you so long?" Tori was panting by the time she reached Frey.

"Holt." Frey grinned.

Frey's answer didn't surprise Tori, so she smiled. Hell, she didn't know why she even asked the question. Of course, Frey had been making love to Holt, just like Tori would be if Alex hadn't left early.

"Where is Mr. wonderful?" Tori looked around.

"He went downstairs to help Alex." Frey looked at her watch. "Do you think they're done? It's a few minutes after eleven."

"I don't know." Tori shrugged.

Frey cracked the door open and spoke from the gap, "Can we come out now?"

"Yes!" Multiple voices screamed.

Frey swung the door open and pushed Tori out first.

"Happy Bridal Shower Day." Everyone screamed at different times.

Tori looked around and saw all the streamers they had hung from one side of the room to the other. There were two decorative chairs under a wide balloon arch made up of different size burnt orange, tan, and off-white balloons. In the center of the arch hung a banner with the words, 'From Miss to Mrs x2'. A table filled with brightly wrapped presents, their ribbons shimmering, stood beside each chair. One table had a 'T' and the other an 'F'. On the other side of the room was another table in front of the gym with a wooden sign propped behind a cake that said, 'Brides to Be'. Off to the side of that table, Tori saw Alex and Holt in front of another table filled with food.

Tori's eyes welled up at the sight of the lovely decorations. Her mom hugged her, then her sister, and so on, until everyone had hugged Frey and Tori. Combining the weddings and showers was a smart move, since the guest lists were almost identical. Not only were Tori's mom and sister at the bridal shower, but so were Sehoy, Isa, Sarah, Maggie, Gaby, Aurora, Minnie, Emmy, and Lucy.

"Hey, baby." Alex was the last one to hug her.

"What are you doing here?" Tori wiped her eyes.

"I wanted to see your face when you saw everything." Alex smiled. "I knew you would love it."

"I do." Tori looked all around. "It's all so beautiful." Tori wrapped her arms around Alex and clung to his neck. "I love you."

"I love you too." Alex held her tightly before releasing her long enough to kiss her temple. "You deserve this and so much more." Alex cupped her face and gently stroked her tears away with his thumbs.

Before Tori could finish speaking, Maggie pulled Alex and Holt toward the elevators. Laughing, Frey draped her arm around Tori's shoulders. Alex and Holt raised their arms in surrender while Maggie shoved them into the elevator. Alex blew Tori a kiss, and Holt winked at Frey.

"See you later, boys." Maggie waved until the elevator doors closed.

Tori figured Maggie stood guard by the elevator so the boys would leave their girl's-only bridal shower.

"I'm hungry, ladies. Let's eat," Isa announced from the food table with a plate already in her hands.

Tori turned with Frey grinning because now that Isa was five months pregnant, she was always hungry. Aurora led Emmy and Lucy to the front of the line, after Isa. Nobody wanted to get between a pregnant woman and her food. After everyone had a full plate, they sat down and were talking nonstop while oohing and aahing at all the food and decorations. Tori's first bridal shower was a resounding success. The joy radiating from her face spoke volumes about how much she enjoyed it. Her face beamed with joy.

Chapter 6

Angel Needs to Learn Her Place...Quick

NUMBERS

"I'm heading to the clubhouse with Steele." Numbers got off the couch when Angel walked out of her room and into the kitchen. He tried to convince her last night to sleep with him after he brought Steele home, but she locked her bedroom door. The thought crossed his mind to break that shit down, but he didn't want to scare Steele. It was important to groom him slowly in the ways of the club.

Soon he would get Angel to marry him and continue Steele's MC education. Yesterday, Steele saw Numbers slap Angel when she walked into their meeting and disrespected him. After the meeting, Steele questioned him about it.

"Why did you hit my mom?" Steele asked as soon as they were alone. Steele, unlike his mother, knew better than to question him in front of his brothers.

"Son, you never let a woman speak to you like that." Numbers sat back in his chair.

"You didn't have to hit her." Steele fidgeted with his fingers on his lap before he mumbled, "My dad never hit her."

"Maybe if he had, she would know her place." Numbers grumbled before he stood. "I'm in charge while your grandfather is in jail. She needs to show me the respect I deserve."

"Won't my grandpa be mad cause you hit his daughter?" Steele frowned at Numbers.

"No. We've talked about my relationship with your mom. Your grandfather approves and wants me to be your dad." Numbers glanced at Steele to see his reaction.

Steele's head jerked up, and he stared wide-eyed at Numbers. "He does?"

"Yep. How do you feel about that?" Numbers couldn't care less if Steele approved or not. He would possess Angel and her sweet body soon.

Steele shrugged and Numbers changed the subject.

"We'll be back later." Numbers announced as he entered the kitchen.

"I have to take him shoe shopping today." Angel continued to stir the scrambled eggs in the pan.

"Take him tomorrow." Numbers walked up behind her, moved her hair aside, and kissed the back of her neck. Angel stepped away with the pan. For a moment, he thought she was going to hit him with it, but she scooped the eggs onto a plate.

"I can't tomorrow. I have something else to do."

Had she heard their plans? "What the fuck do you have to do on a Sunday, and New Year's Eve, no less?" Numbers pulled the pan out of her hand and dropped it into the sink.

"I have to meet with a client."

"On a fucking Sunday?" Numbers jerked her against his body, gripping her ass to hold her in place.

Angel placed her hands against his chest, attempting to keep her distance. *Stupid girl. Did she think she could get out of his embrace?*

"It's a new client, and that's the only day she could meet."

"Then I'll keep Steele today and tomorrow." Numbers ran one hand up her back and mashed her breasts into his chest while he licked and sucked her neck.

"No." Angel struggled. "You can take him today, but I'll keep him tomorrow."

"We'll see." Numbers gripped a handful of her hair near her scalp, preventing her from moving her head as he took control of her mouth. Initially, she resisted, but after he bit her bottom lip forcefully and she gasped, he seized the opportunity to enter. In time, she would learn to follow his orders.

"Mom?"

Numbers released her, but not before giving her a warning glare.

Angel ran to Steele for a hug. "How about some breakfast and then we'll go shopping for shoes?"

"Woman, I told you I'm taking him today." Numbers pulled her away from Steele and shoved her aside. "I'll bring him back tonight. Get dressed Steele so we can leave."

"Mom?" Steele's questioning gaze toward his mom caused Numbers to face her, daring her to defy him.

"It's fine. You can go with Numbers. We'll uh...go shopping tomorrow."

"Okay." Steele turned and left the room.

"If you ever try that again, I will beat the shit out of you." Numbers got in her face. "Don't fucking test me, Angel. You won't like the devil you raise."

"Whatever." Angel stared at him with disgust.

Bitch better listen to me. Numbers swung up and punched her so hard she fell back against the sink. Angel turned around, her eyes wide with a mixture of shock and fear, staring at him. The swelling around her eye had already turned a disturbing shade of purple, almost completely closing it. *Why did she keep making me hit her?*

"Mom, what happened?" Steele ran back into the kitchen and toward her.

"She tripped and hit her face on the counter." Numbers grabbed Steele and pulled him toward the door. The last thing he needed was for Steele to see his mom crying. "We need to go. We're burning daylight. I'll bring him back tonight." Numbers yelled when he opened the front door.

"Where are we going?" Steele asked.

"To the club." Numbers held out a helmet for Steele. He was the future president and as such, Numbers needed to keep him safe.

"Okay."

Numbers got on the bike, waiting for Steele to buckle his helmet. "Hop on and hang tight."

Numbers pulled out, never giving Angel a second glance. That would teach her to defy his orders. It was time to get to the clubhouse and work on a plan to kill those two bitches.

Chapter 7

Chippendale Who?

BARRETT

"Okay, boys!" Alex hollered when he and Holt entered the suite Barrett had reserved for them to practice their striptease. "The girls are enjoying the bridal shower. We have about three to four hours to practice our routine." Alex thrust his hips forward.

"And eat." Barrett blurted out and raised the menu up in the air. Everyone stared at him. "What?" Barrett shrugged. "I'm hungry. I say we order room service and practice until it gets here."

"Sounds good to me," Mark agreed.

Alex grabbed the menu from Barrett and passed it around until everyone chose their meal.

Barrett let Alex handle the food order while he connected his phone to his mini speaker. The boys agreed to use the song "It's Raining Men" by The Weather Girls. They figured if Magic Mike stripped to it in his movie, then they could too. Barrett was relieved he didn't have a girl in the mix and didn't have to be a part of the show. These guys were crazy to agree to strip. Didn't they know strippers practiced a lot before they did their routines in front of sex craved women?

"Okay, who watched Magic Mike to get some moves?" Barrett looked around the room. Some nodded their heads, but not everyone. Amateurs. The girls were going to eat them alive.

"Did you guys bring your outfits?" Alex looked at everyone.

"Yep, they're all here." Barrett shook his head. "I put them in the master bedroom. Did you bring yours?"

Alex was wearing slacks and a button-down shirt. "Considering I only need my apron," Alex said as he held up his hand with his black apron and hat, "yep."

"Holt and I saw the setup when we delivered the food to the girls. Tori and Frey had designated chairs on that side of the room." Alex pointed to his right. "The rest of the girls fit on the couch and love seat facing them. I told my mom Tommy was coming with Skip around two to swim in the pool. I told her we had a surprise for the girls and wanted her to take Aurora, Dyani, Lizzy, Minnie, Emmy, and Lucy downstairs around that time. She promised to text me when the party was wrapping up so we could come up."

"I invited Bryce and the shelter boys." Holt nodded. "Tim will drive them over."

"I'm glad you invited them." Thunder smiled. "They love coming over and swimming in the pool."

"Skip said he and Minnie are taking the kids back to their ranch for a sleepover after swimming." Grayhorse told everyone.

"They're going to babysit all the kids?" Matteo asked, dumbfounded.

"Yep." Grayhorse nodded. "They never had kids and love being around all of ours. Besides, Minnie was afraid Lilly wouldn't want to sleep in the playpen. This way, if she gets fussy, she can take her next door to our house and stay with her there while Skip watches the older kids."

Barrett needed to get this party started. They were wasting precious time, so he clapped his hands. "Okay, gentlemen. Who needs help with their routine?"

"Are you volunteering to help us?" Alex quirked his eyebrow.

Barrett was a good dancer, but Matteo and Mark were the best dancers in the group. "No. I figured Mark and Matteo could help whoever needed dance moves, or I could play the movie Magic Mike or any other YouTube videos to teach you moves."

"Are we dancing throughout the entire song?" Holt asked.

"The single version is only a little over three minutes." Barrett looked it up on his phone.

"I guess if we get the girls all revved up, we can always get them to dance with us so we're not the only ones dancing." Matteo crossed his arms and looked at the boys.

"How much are we taking off?" Thunder pointed at Grayhorse. "He's with my sister. I'm not sure I want to strip down to nothing in front of my sister."

"Ditto." Matteo smirked at Thunder.

"We are not getting naked." Alex was adamant. "We can get down to pants or boxers, whichever you prefer."

Barrett checked his watch and noticed almost an hour had passed since they got their shit together. "We're losing precious time, so let's move some of this furniture to what Holt and Alex saw and let's practice."

Everyone helped Alex move the furniture to match the setup at the bridal shower.

Barrett connected his phone to the TV and got their attention. "I have some videos from that tick app if any of you want to learn the hip move, body roll, dice walk, throw it back, bust down, and the dolphin."

"What the fuck is he talking about?" Grayhorse asked Thunder.

"I have no fucking clue. It all sounds like gibberish to me."

Barrett smiled, knowing once they saw the moves, they would understand the names. He cued up the video called 'Top Ten Moves' and watched their faces. It was fucking hysterical seeing the boys trying some moves as they watched the guy on the TV. After the video ended, they asked to watch several of the moves again until they figured out their routine. When they were ready, Barrett hit play on his song's app, and the boys practiced putting their dance moves together. Barrett crossed his arms and covered his mouth with one hand so they wouldn't see him laughing at them.

Matteo was slaying his dance moves, swaying his hips to a spicy salsa rhythm and adding in some body rolls. *Must be nice to have that Latin blood flowing through your veins.* Mark blended many dances like the salsa, body rolls, dice walk, throw it back, and the fucker even did the dolphin, which required some serious core strength. *Damn, he was good. Thank fuck, Mark was taken because he would give him a run for his money at a bar if he was his wingman.*

Grayhorse looked like he was doing the hula hoop with some added hip rolls and body rolls. *Huh, did he bring a hula hoop?* Thunder was doing the men's fancy dance interspersed with hip rolls, body rolls, and dice walk. *Nice choreography. He wouldn't have believed it if he hadn't seen it.* Barrett didn't realize someone could make the fancy dance that provocative.

Alex was doing slow hip and body rolls as he scooted closer to the couch. Barrett guessed he was going to gyrate his cock in Tori's face. *Tori would definitely blush.* She was shier than the other girls. *Who knew his older bro had moves?* Holt spread his legs out before he dropped onto the floor in a push-up position and did a full body roll. Then he jumped up into a wide sitting position and thrust his hips repeatedly. *Who knew he was that agile? Frey was going to love that. Fuck, what was he thinking?* The last thing Barrett wanted was to see his friend's moves on his sister.

"Okay." Barrett shouted when the song ended. "I hate to say it, but you guys did good. Not that you turned me on or anything." All the guys were staring at him funny as they were breathing heavy, some more than others. "Fuck! Don't look at me like that. You know what I mean."

They all busted out laughing.

"Assholes." Barrett mumbled as he got ready to start the song again. "Go get your damn costumes on so you can figure out what you are taking off and when. Remember, no nudists." Barrett wore his work clothes because as soon as he finished his emcee gig, he had to work the casino floor.

They laughed at Barrett as they went into the bedroom to get their costumes. All except Alex. He already had his chef stuff.

"Seriously, how did we look?" Alex put his arm around him.

"Are you fucking with me?" Barrett got out from under his arm.

"No. Seriously." Alex put on his apron. "Do you think we can pull this off without the girls laughing at us?"

"Yeah, I don't think they'll be laughing, especially when your clothes come flying off." Barrett smirked at him. *Was Alex fucking serious?* Those girls were going to eat this up, and he was going to have to leave before the orgy started.

They all came back into the room and had time to practice once before the food got there. After they ate, they ran through the dance a couple more times before Sehoy texted Alex.

"Show time boys." Alex hollered. "That was my mom. The bridal shower is over. Let's roll."

Barrett gathered his phone and speaker, locking the door after everyone left the room. Several guests gawked at them as they walked down the hallway to the elevator. Well, they did look like a modern version of the Village People.

Barrett felt a tug on his arm and stopped short. Turning, he looked down at an older lady wearing way too much makeup.

"Are you guys performing tonight?" the lady looked eagerly at him while her eyes roamed his body. Her hand rubbing up and down his arm.

"Uh, no." Barrett looked at the guys for an assist, but they were too busy elbowing each other and laughing at him. "We are rehearsing. Maybe we'll perform in the future."

"Ooh, sounds good." The old lady grabbed his butt, causing him to jump, and then she turned to look at the guys. "I'll keep an eye out for it. I bet you're all excellent dancers."

Barrett's body shuttered when she licked her lips after staring at the guys and walked away.

"Now, that's," –Matteo pointed in the old lady's direction– "just wrong. She's older than my mom."

"Yeah, that was fuckin' creepy." Mark pushed the elevator button several times. "Let's hope she doesn't come back before the elevator gets here."

"No Shit." Barrett and the guys faced the elevator doors. He was sure they were all praying for that beautiful ding sound.

Ding

"Thank fuck." Holt sighed, and they all rushed into the elevator. It was a quick ride to the family floor. Barrett could see them adjusting their costumes and shaking out their arms, preparing for their performance. Once again, he was grateful he didn't have a girlfriend.

When the doors opened on their floor, Barrett got ready to step out, but froze in the elevator doorway. *Oh shit.* Emmy, Lucy and the moms were facing the elevator, staring at them. Barrett was so shocked the elevator doors hit him when they attempted to close, jerking him out of his stupor.

"Hey, ladies. What are you still doing here?" Barrett stared at this mom.

Sehoy coughed into her hand, hiding her laugh. "We're leaving now to go to the pool."

Barrett stepped out and placed his hands on the elevator door as the boys got out. Their girls were staring at them with lust in their eyes and mouths open. Oh yeah, this was going to be great.

"*Lekší!*" Lucy shrieked and ran to Thunder. Thunder braced himself and caught her. "Why are you in your pow-wow regalia?"

"Uh. I need Isa to let me know if it looked good." Thunder's lip twitched and he looked nervous.

"Dad?" Emmy wore a puzzled frown.

Time to save them and scoot the others out. "Okay, mom." Barrett gently assisted Sehoy into the elevator. "You guys have fun."

"*¡Ay, Dios mío! ¡Qué guapos! Dale, mi niña.*" Aurora took Lucy from Thunder's arms. "Let's go swimming. You can see your uncle tomorrow."

"But, *Abuela*, I wanna stay and put on a costume too." Lucy whined from Aurora's arms.

"I gotta see this." Lizzy stood with her arms crossed and a wide grin on her face.

"This is not for you, young lady." Dyani shoved Lizzy from behind into the elevator.

"But mom." Lizzy rolled her eyes.

"You can pick up your kids in the morning from my house." Minnie said on her way into the elevator.

"Bye." Barrett waved as the doors closed.

"Fuck, okay." As Barrett turned to look in the room, he saw the boys smiling at the girls perched on the edge of their seats. "Ladies, stay seated. We have a show for you."

"I love shows!" Maggie shouted and clapped her hands.

Barrett started the song. When the first note hit, the boys sauntered over to their girl and began their dance. All except Mark. He moonwalked to Maggie and twerked before he began all his moves. Barrett watched Maggie smile and lick her lips. *Oh yeah, Mark was getting lucky tonight.*

Barrett was grateful to see Grayhorse had a lasso, not a hula hoop. Not that it mattered. He could have a fucking pink princess inflatable pool float around his waist and Sarah would still be eye fucking him.

As the refrain played, they tore off their hats and shirts. Thunder bent down and placed his headdress in Isa's lap. Then he executed an impressive body roll as he pulled his buckskin shirt over his head and threw it at her, and winked. That shirt had special meaning for them. She ran out on him during one of his cultural center openings while wearing only that shirt and her panties. Barrett wasn't there, but he'd heard the story from Alex.

Barrett's mouth dropped when Mark ripped his dress shirt off, and buttons went flying everywhere. *Go Mark.* But the best part was watching Maggie's eyes widen. *Guess he'd never done that before.* Holt must have bought a stripper cop outfit because he just ripped that shirt open, but buttons didn't fly. The impact wasn't any different from the lustful look on his sister's face. *Shit, he couldn't watch them. That was just gross.*

Barrett turned away and glanced at Alex, now without an apron and only in a speedo. *Oh shit*, he was approaching Tori while he thrusted his pelvis toward her. *Yep, he called it. Tori was blushing and covered her face. But wait, was she peeking? Her fingers slid further apart, and Barrett could see her eyes staring at Alex's crotch and abs—that speedo hid nothing. Alex would turn her into his sex kitten in no time.*

When the song said 'God bless mother nature' the rest of the boys either ripped off their pants or let them drop to the floor. Holt, Thunder, and Grayhorse were wearing speedo bathing suits, like Alex. Must've been Thunder's idea since he wore those under his buckskins when he did field trips to hide his goods from young impressionable girls and their moms. Yep, Alex had told him that story, too.

Barrett heard Maggie's laughter and turned toward them. Matteo and Mark were wearing boxers. *What the fuck was Mark wearing?* He had red boxers with white hearts and in big bold letters were the words 'Big Sexy' across his ass. Barrett was sure there was a story behind those boxers from the way Maggie was laughing. Mark placed his thumbs under the waistband and pretended to lower it. Yup, that stopped her mid-laugh.

Now, all the boys were approaching their girls and either giving them lap dances or pulling them up to dance with them while they kissed the shit out of them. It was time for Barrett to leave. But first, he had to approach Thunder, Grayhorse, and Matteo. Though he felt foolish interrupting, he wanted to offer them their Chippendale rehearsal room key for a romantic evening. Luckily, they were dancing near each other.

"Boys, here's the keycard to that suite we practiced in, so you don't have to go home." Barrett held the key at eye level between two fingers. "It has two master bedrooms and a couch. Anyone want it?"

"Uh, not me. I don't want to be loving my woman with my sister in the next bedroom." Thunder smirked at Grayhorse.

"Me, neither." Matteo grabbed Gaby's hips and pulled her closer.

"I'll drive home. Isa is more comfortable at home in our bed." Thunder kissed her forehead. "You guys take it, since you rarely get a night away from your kids."

"*Pilámaya*." Grayhorse nodded at Thunder. "We'll take it."

"We'll stay too." Matteo wiggled his eyebrows at Gaby.

Barrett handed it to Grayhorse.

"Matteo, you ready to go?" Grayhorse held the keycard up.

"Yep," Matteo nodded.

"*Tibló*," Sarah hugged Thunder. "We'll return the favor after your baby arrives and you guys need a night off."

"*Pilámaya*." Thunder put his arm around Isa, and they headed to the couch for his clothing.

"Well, my work is done." Barrett lifted his arm and shouted. "Great job, guys. Gotta go, some of us have to work tonight." He headed to the elevator with Thunder, Grayhorse, Matteo, and their girls. But he heard Holt say, "I'm gonna be working too. Pleasing your sister." *Motherfucker, I didn't need that image in my head.*

Chapter 8

I Hate Numbers

ANGEL

After Numbers left with Steele, Angel drove by the cultural center, hoping maybe someone would be there and could help her get in touch with Tori or anyone else in the wedding party, but it was closed. The sign said the center would reopen after the new year, but that would be too late. The wedding is tomorrow night, New Year's Eve! With no other option, and still in so much pain from Numbers' punch, she headed home.

Once home, she took more ibuprofen and laid on the couch with an ice pack because her face was throbbing. She must've dozed because it was now almost dinnertime and Steele wasn't home. Angel despised the fact that Steele was with Numbers, and would now be in on the plan to kill Maggie and Tori. She felt so helpless.

She couldn't believe that asshole had forced her to kiss him and then punched her. Numbers was getting dangerous. She needed to get Steele and get out of town. But where would she go? She didn't have any family that she knew of, and she would have to change her name or Numbers would find her.

How could she convince Steele to leave with her when he was always with Numbers? She had to come up with a plan. She would need to get some cash and make a list of everything she needed. Numbers would notice if she started packing. Maybe she could pack the essentials and hide the suitcases in her car. Once Steele was back in school, she could check him out early one day and drive out of town. The earlier in the morning, the better. It would give her a good head start before school was out and Numbers got suspicious.

Angel's heart was pounding as hard as her face at the thought of all this deception. It was getting dark. Where was Steele? Should she go to the clubhouse and get him? Grabbing her phone, she called Numbers.

"What do you want?" Numbers answered.

Angel could hear whooping and hollering in the background. Were they having a party?

"Where's Steele? When are you bringing him home?"

"He's staying here tonight."

"No!" Angel hollered.

"You don't tell me what to do, bitch. You need to learn your place."

"Bring him home right now or I'm coming to get him." Angel got off the couch, heading toward the door.

"If you come here, I'll fucking beat the shit out of you and pass you around." Angel froze in place and shivered at the fury in Number's voice. "I'll bring him home tomorrow."

She believed him. "Okay."

There was nothing left to say. Not that it mattered, Numbers hung up. He was drunk and angry. She bolted her front door and ran to her room. Grabbing Tools' gun from the gun safe, she crawled into bed with the gun under her pillow. She hated guns, but if Numbers came by tonight to hurt her, she would be ready.

Chapter 9

Gotta Save My Sister

JOSÉ

"*El Loco!*" Manuel ran into the Los Lobos Clubhouse yelling, then stopped in front of José while bending over, trying to catch his breath.

"*¿Manuel, que paso?*" José was drinking a beer at the bar with Machete, the Los Lobos president, when he saw Manuel. Something must have spooked him because Manuel never ran anywhere.

"I just heard–" Manuel stood and held his chest "–the LRs...are planning... a shootout ... at your sister's friend's wedding...today."

"What the fuck are you talking about?" José and Machete bolted off their bar stools.

"What did you hear?" Machete waved the other brothers over.

"I was at the gas station when I overheard one of their prospects running his mouth about how they were going to teach those two bitches a lesson. The other prospect told him to shut his mouth, but he kept going. It sounded like they are planning to kill your sister, and another girl named Tori, at a wedding at that gambling resort tonight."

"Fuck!" José reached for his phone. "I need to warn Maggie."

"There's no time." Machete grabbed his hand and looked around at all the brothers who were present. "Get everyone here...NOW! We must prepare to protect Maggie and her friends."

This is not the way José wanted to end the year. If anything happened to Maggie again, it would kill him. Hell, what happened to Lola, his lover, was slowly taking away his sanity one day at a time. Lucifer's Renegades were going to pay for the hell they had caused Maggie and Lola. He would kill as many as he could tonight without remorse. Enough was enough. He didn't care about himself anymore, but his sister needed to live a full and happy life. He tried to call Maggie and Mark, but both calls went straight to voicemail.

Chapter 10

Brides/Grooms Gifts

BARRETT

T he day of his sister's wedding had finally arrived. Barrett knew Frey was bouncing off the walls, ready to walk down the aisle and be with Holt forever – it was a twin thing with them, this connection with their thoughts and feelings.

Barrett wasn't happy about getting kicked out of his room, but Sehoy had claimed the family floor for the girls and had reserved a suite on another floor for Alex, Holt, and the groomsmen. Next thing he knew, he was on the elevator with his toiletries and tux. Because the boys prepared faster than the girls, they chilled in the living room of their suite before getting dressed.

The wedding party couples were Isa and Thunder, Sarah and Grayhorse, Maggie and Mark, Gaby and Matteo, and Barrett was paired off with Lizzy. They had two flower girls: Emmy and Lucy. *Thank fuck, Lucy wasn't doing their hair, or the wedding photos would be very interesting. Lucy had a history of experimenting with hair. Although, that might be a fun look, not for a wedding.* They also had two ring bearers. Tommy was Alex's and Bryce was Holt's.

"Hey, Barrett." Alex and Holt called him over. "Can you take these presents to Frey and Tori?"

"Of course." Barrett grabbed the small bags and wondered what the boys had bought them.

When he reached Frey's room, he knocked on their door and called out. "Hey, it's Barrett."

Maggie whipped the door open. "Hey, Barrett. What's up?"

"The boys have gifts for their girls, and they wanted me to deliver them." Barrett held the two bags out for Maggie to take them.

"That's so sweet." Maggie took the bags. "Come in, but stay here. Some girls are only in their robes." Maggie spun around and left with the bags.

Barrett stared at the floor, not wanting to look up and embarrass anyone, especially himself. Normally, he would love to catch girls in their robes, but these girls had boys that would kick his ass if he saw something he shouldn't.

"I'm back." Maggie was carrying two boxes. "These are from the girls for the boys."

Barrett was ready to take the packages when Frey and Tori came running around the corner with rollers in half of their hair. He could thank Lucy for even knowing what rollers were.

"Oh my God, Barrett. Tell Holt, I love it!" Frey threw herself into his arms before he could get the gifts from Maggie. "Give him a hug and kiss from me."

"Uh, yeah, that's a hard no." Barrett hugged her but shook his head. "You can thank him after the ceremony."

"Okay." Frey stepped back, smiling at him. "Fair enough."

"Can you please tell Alex I love it and thank you?" Tori gave him a quick hug.

"Absolutely." Barrett was glad Tori was comfortable enough to hug him. After what Winston did to her, she was leery of men, especially if they touched her.

"What did they give you?" Barrett quirked an eyebrow. "I never saw the gifts."

Frey pointed to the necklace she was wearing. "Holt got me this necklace and charm."

The heart-shaped charm, encircled by diamonds and engraved with "My Heart, My Love, My Everything," caught Barrett's eye. He flipped it over and saw the wedding date engraved on it. Damn, Holt was becoming a pussy.

"He's so whipped." Barrett murmured and earned a smack on his shoulder by Frey.

"What did Alex get you, Tori?" Barrett looked at Tori.

Tori pushed her hair back and showed him large diamond earrings. "Alex always says I need to sparkle like the gorgeous, strong woman I am and stop hiding. I'd say these are big and sparkly."

"Yeah, those are beautiful, but not as beautiful as you." Barrett inwardly winced. He knew Winston had called Tori beautiful. They all tried to stay away from that word, but he slipped. *Shit, he felt bad.* But wait, she didn't even flinch. *Damn, he was so proud of her.* Tori was gaining her strength and confidence a little more every day. It probably helped that Frey was her best friend, and they hung out together all the time. Frey didn't take shit from anybody.

"Thank you, Barrett." Tori grabbed his wrists and pulled him down to give him a kiss on the cheek.

Alex was a lucky man. He got a sweet one.

"You're welcome, sis." After today, Tori would be his sister-in-law. Watching Tori, he saw her get teary-eyed. Barrett gave her a quick hug and headed to the door. "I'll take those to the boys." Barrett pointed to the gifts that Maggie still held.

"You know what?" Lizzy came around the corner in her robe and grabbed the gifts from Maggie's hand. "I'll take them to the boys. I want to see their reactions so I can tell my sister if her new hubby liked his gift."

"Fair enough. Come with me." Barrett held the door open for her to step through. "I'll see you ladies later."

Barrett watched Lizzy sashay to the elevator. *Was she trying to flirt with him?* She was younger than his usual type. Besides, he wasn't ready to settle down and he couldn't fuck around with Tori's sister. She was family and most definitely off limits!

Lizzy held the elevator door open for Barrett and winked at him. *Fuck, this was going to get ugly if he didn't nip it in the bud.* He had to make sure she understood he wasn't interested.

"So." Barrett started the conversation as he stepped as far away from her as possible in such a small enclosure. "Pretty exciting that our siblings are marrying today, huh? It'll be nice to have two more sisters in the family." Barrett hoped she could read between the lines, but just in case, he continued to clear the blurred lines. "You and Tori already feel like little sisters to me." *Yep, that did it.* Out of the corner of his eye, Barrett watched Lizzy's body deflate while her sexy smile turned into a frown. Barrett hoped he wasn't too harsh with his comment.

"Yeah, having a couple of brothers will be awesome." Lizzy said with no enthusiasm in her voice.

Barrett led her to the boy's suite and held the door open for her.

"Lizzy's here with presents for Alex and Holt." Barrett hollered before she reached the living room. He wasn't worried about Lizzy seeing them naked since everyone was in shorts and a t-shirt when he left. At most, he'd been gone for half an hour.

"Hey, Lizzy." Rising from the couch, Alex went to greet her. "How's Tori?"

"She's great. She loved her gift." Lizzy turned to Holt. "Frey loved hers, too. You guys did a fantastic job. I brought yours to report back to them. Can you open them now? I need to get back and finish getting ready. Barrett," –Lizzy pointed over her shoulder to Barrett– "can give you all the details after I leave."

"Absolutely." Alex reached for his present at the same time Holt said 'sure' and got his.

Barrett watched Alex unwrap his box and open the lid. Alex pulled out a card and read it out loud.

"In Lakota culture, the buffalo (also called "Tatanka") is the animal most strongly associated with protection, as it provided sustenance, shelter, and was a sacred being that gave itself freely to the people, representing the importance of sharing and providing for others, making it a symbol of life and abundance. This embodies everything you are to me. I love you, Tori." Alex pulled out the Buffalo necklace on a braided leather cord. "Barrett, will you put this around my neck? I want to wear it for Tori." Alex turned around and handed Barrett the necklace. "Lizzy, please tell Tori I love her, and I can't wait to marry her. I will always be her safe shelter."

Holt opened his box and grinned at Frey's note.

"Why do you have a shit-eating grin on your face?" Barrett frowned at Holt.

"Frey's note." Holt held it up and read it. "So, you can watch over me and stop fucking me so I can be on time. I love you, Frey."

"Oh, fuck no. She didn't write that." Barrett dropped his head and shook it.

"Read it and weep, bro." Holt held the card out for Barrett to read it.

"Nope." Barrett raised his arms and stepped back. "I'm gonna pretend you never said those words."

Holt pulled the nice leather band watch out of the box and turned it over. "It says Love Always, Frey, and our wedding date."

"You should've gotten her a watch." Barrett smiled. "She's always fucking late."

"How right you are. Sometimes she's late because we're fucking." Holt chuckled and wiggled his eyebrows at Barrett.

"Shut the fuck up, man!" Barrett punched Holt's shoulder. "I don't need to hear that."

Alex smacked him on the back of his head like he always did since they were kids. *Good,* Barrett thought. *Maybe now he'd shut the fuck up about having sex with my sister.*

"Ow!" Holt shouted and rubbed the back of his head. After putting on the watch, he gave Lizzy a hug. "Please, tell Frey I love it and give her a hug for me."

"Will do." Lizzy smiled at Holt, but turned to Barrett. Her eyes travelled over his body, but luckily, she left before saying anything.

"What the hell was that about?" Holt never missed much. Thank fuck, Alex had already walked away to show Thunder his necklace.

"What are you talking about?" Barrett tried to play off the stupid card.

Holt crossed his arms and lowered his voice. "Don't play dumb with me. She fucking undressed you with her eyes. Are you fucking crazy? She is about to be your sister-in-law. Alex will kill you if you fuck with her."

"Like I almost killed you for fucking with *our* sister." Barrett glared at Holt. Holt, of all people, should know he would never cross that line.

"Shut the fuck up." Holt pointed his finger in Barrett's face and whispered. "Just cause your family took care of me doesn't make her *my* sister. Today is not the day to bring up this shit again."

When Holt and Frey hooked up, Barrett was not amused, and he almost screwed up his friendship with Holt because of his dumb promises.

"You're right." Barrett sighed. "I'm just fucking with you."

"Fucker." Holt smiled at Barrett. "What about her?"

"She was flirting with me in the elevator." Barrett watched Alex as he joked with Thunder. *Was he going to have to be blunt with Lizzy?* Alex would beat the shit out of him if he hurt Tori's sister. Barrett rarely turned girls down. He either ignored them until they walked away, or he went along with their games, slept with them, and never called. *Damn, now that Holt was with Frey, he'd turned into the man whore.* His mother would be so disappointed in him.

"Seriously, though." Holt slapped the back of his hand on Barrett's chest to get his attention. "Are you interested in her?"

"Nope, not even a little bit." Barrett shook his head. "I thought I let her down easy in the elevator before we got here, but I guess I wasn't clear enough. I mean," –Barrett attempting to lighten the mood before Alex caught wind of their conversation and motioned toward his body with his hand– "who could resist this hot body?"

"Just fucking watch yourself." Holt grumbled and went back to the couch to watch TV.

Barrett released a deep breath. Yeah, he needed to make sure Lizzy didn't get any crazy ideas.

Chapter 11

Best Day of My Life

Frey

Frey stared at her reflection, overwhelmed with happiness at the prospect of marrying her best friend and soulmate. She would never have pictured herself in a wedding dress marrying Holt just a month prior. They had endured countless trials, but nothing compared to the gut-wrenching grief of losing their child. A wave of sadness washed over her as she placed her hands on her stomach. A child she hadn't realized she was carrying until it was too late. With their whole lives stretching out before them, full of hope and dreams, they agreed to try for another baby. But for now, she would concentrate on adopting Bryce and creating a home filled with laughter and family for him.

Lucky for them, Holt's mother was no longer an issue. She stabbed Frey and received a twenty-five-year prison sentence. The judge gave her a stiffer sentence because of the abuse she caused Holt throughout his childhood. Sighing, she shook her head. Enough with those thoughts. Today was all about happy thoughts and new beginnings.

She couldn't wait to walk down the aisle with her father and see Holt waiting for her. She wondered if he would cry. There were lots of videos that showed the groom crying when he watched his bride walking down the aisle. Would Holt cry or smile? Frey couldn't wait to find out.

"*Chackshosti*, you look beautiful." Sehoy came up behind Frey and gave her a gentle hug.

Looking at her mom's glassy eyes through the mirror, Frey felt tears welling up in her eyes.

"Thank you, *chatski*." Frey turned to face her mom. "Please don't cry or you'll make me cry and I'll have to redo my makeup."

"My heart is bursting with joy for you today. My beautiful, strong, confident girl who makes me so proud to be her mother. You couldn't have picked a better husband. He is lucky to have you. Your love has blossomed over the past few weeks, making your father and I so happy for you both. I realize you might have more obstacles in your future, but we know together you will overcome them. We love you." Sehoy squeezed Frey's hands.

"*Chatski*, you said you would not make me cry." Frey tilted her head back, hoping to keep the tears at bay.

"I'm done with the sappy stuff." Sehoy stepped back and handed Frey a tissue. "I'll help you with your shoes and then we can see how Tori's doing."

"Okay." Frey dabbed her eyes lightly, getting the tears before they streamed down her cheeks. Her parents had always showered her with their love. Today was no different. She silently prayed she wouldn't dissolve into a blubbering mess when her father led her down the aisle.

*** Tori ***

Tori's mom and sister were helping her get dressed in Holt's old room. Only a few of Tori's tribal council members could attend her wedding because they lived in South Dakota. Alex, ever the wonderful man, promised to take her to her reservation after their honeymoon. Fortunately, Spirit of the Eagle, a Lakota Medicine Man and Oglala Lakota Tribal Elder, agreed to be the officiant of their weddings. Thunder and Sarah called him Uncle Spirit because he had been Thunder's father's best friend who helped raise Sarah after they lost their parents in a horrible car accident.

Tori was marrying the kindest man she'd ever met, aside from her father. Alex's love supported her during her encounters with Winston and empowered her to embrace her inner strength as a warrior instead of a victim. With each passing day, she felt a greater sense of strength and confidence within herself.

Before Dyani could attach the veil into the back of her bun, Tori hiked up her skirt and twirled around, making Dyani and Lizzy laugh.

"*Cuŋwítku*, stop before you make yourself dizzy." Dyani smiled at her.

"I am so happy, *iná*." Tori screamed, grabbed her mom, and hugged her.

"I know you are, but you are going to ruin your hair if you keep acting crazy." Dyani stepped back.

"This is not like you." Lizzy pointed at her. "You're the quiet, calm one."

"Not today." Tori squeezed Lizzy and jumped up and down. "Today, I am the happiest person on earth because I'm going to marry the man of my dreams."

"Hey, what's all the shouting about?" Maggie ran into the room.

"She's lost it." Lizzy pulled away from Tori and looked at her like she'd lost her marbles.

"Nope, sister dear, I've found it!" Tori was beaming at them.

"Found what?" Maggie quirked an eyebrow and whispered to Lizzy. "What did she lose?"

"Her mind." Lizzy said out of the corner of her mouth.

"Stay still *cuŋwítku,* so I can put the veil on your bun." Dyani held the veil in her hand.

Tori stopped moving and slightly bent down so her mom could attach the veil. Dyani spread it around her back and laid it out before stepping around to stare at her daughter.

"You look stunning. I am so proud of you. You left home and have created your own path. You are stronger than you think, and I'm so glad you are finally seeing your inner strength. I will always be grateful to Alex for helping you get there." Dyani reached for her daughter's hands. "Let's go out there and hold hands. I want to pray together with our family and friends."

Lizzy picked up Tori's train and followed her into the living room. Frey, Gaby, Isa, Sarah, Aurora, Emmy, and Lucy were already waiting for them. As soon as Frey saw Tori, they both screamed and ran to each other. Holding hands, they took small jumps as they squealed with delight.

"Okay, ladies simmer down." Dyani grabbed their hands. "Let's all form a circle and hold hands. I'd like to say our Lakota Wedding Prayer for Tori and Frey." Everyone joined hands and bowed their heads.

Dyani took a deep breath and closed her eyes before she began. "Teach me how to trust my heart, my mind, my intuition, my inner knowing, the senses of my body, the blessings of my spirit. Teach me to trust these things so that I may enter my sacred space and love beyond my fear and thus walk in balance with the passing of each glorious sun. *Wakan Tanka*, please bless these two unions."

"I would like to add one of our prayers, if I may?" Sehoy said when Dyani finished.

They all murmured their acceptance.

"Now, you will feel no rain, for each of you will be shelter for the other. Now, you will feel no cold, for each of you will be warmth to the other. Now, there will be no loneliness, for each of you will be a companion to the other. Now, you are two persons, but there is only one life before you." Sehoy squeezed Frey's hand.

"That was beautiful, *chatski*. Thank you." Frey kissed her mom's cheek.

Knock, Knock.

Everyone turned to the door, but Maggie was the first to answer it.

Tori saw her father and Mr. Panther coming toward them with huge smiles on their faces. They looked so handsome in their black tuxedos with crisp white shirts.

"Well, don't you both look absolutely stunning." Tall Bear walked up to Tori and gave her a hug.

"*Pilámaya, até*," Tori said into the crook of Tall Bear's neck.

"Are you girls ready?" Osceola gave Frey a kiss on her cheek. "We're ready to escort you to your future husbands."

After lots of yeses, they all grabbed the flower bouquets and headed out.

Chapter 12

Wedding Day

BARRETT

Thank fuck, his dad had paid overtime to get this Convention Center/Wedding Venue finished in time for today. Barrett didn't think they were going to make it with Christmas being so close to the wedding. But the contractor finished the outside a week ago and everyone concentrated on the inside. The workers were ecstatic to get a bigger paycheck before Christmas. Holt, Alex, Mark, Thunder, Grayhorse, and Barrett volunteered to help during their time off from work with the construction while Isa, Maggie, Frey, Tori, Lizzy, Dyani, Sehoy and an interior decorator put the finishing touches on the interior spaces. Their hard work had clearly paid off–the venue was beautiful.

The groomsmen, dressed in black tuxedos, seated everyone. Since it was a double wedding and the guests knew both couples, there was no need to seat the bride's guests on one side and the groom's guests on the other side; this was a combined wedding in every sense. In attendance were family, friends, the shelter boys, some employees, the Seminole Tribe of Florida Tribal Council, some of the Lakota Tribal Council, and security.

Lucifer's Renegades had been too quiet these last couple of days. Not one to take any chances, Barrett made sure some of their security officers were upstairs along with Deputy George, Deputy Sean, K-9 Deputy Bryan with Sky, and some other undercover deputies. Some officers were downstairs, while others sat among the guests.

"Hey, man." Barrett slapped Deputy George on the back. "How's it going?"

"Ah, the Best Man!" Deputy George turned and smiled. "All good. We checked things out before we came up and everything was quiet so far."

"Thanks, man. I appreciate your help." Barrett shook Deputy Sean's hand. "Hopefully, you guys can stay long enough to eat some food." Barrett also greeted Deputy Bryan. "Thanks for bringing Sky. Mark will be happy to see her."

"No worries. She's a fantastic officer." Deputy Bryan reached down, giving Sky the signal to sit. "I took her over to Mark a few minutes ago so he could see her."

Barrett felt his phone buzz and looked at the message from Sehoy telling him they were ready.

"Gotta run and get this show on the road. See you boys later." Barrett jogged up to Alex and Holt. "Everyone's ready. I'll walk Uncle Spirit to the altar. Holt, please help Mom to her seat. Alex, you seat Tori's mom."

"Good plan." Alex nodded. "I was wondering how we were going to do this."

"The ladies left it up to me, and I thought this was the best idea." Barrett felt confident in his decision since Holt's birth mother was no longer a part of his life. Holt told Barrett that after his birth father kicked them out and his mother started doing drugs, he never thought of her as his mom. She was Betty to him. Sehoy was his chosen mom, and Holt was grateful for everything she had done for him. So, on this special day, it made sense to have Holt escort Sehoy and since Tori didn't have a brother, Alex would escort Dyani. "I'm gonna go signal the DJ and bring our moms to you guys. Stay here." Barrett pointed at them. "No peeking at the brides."

Alex and Holt held up their hands, shook their heads, and smiled at him.

"Thanks, bro." Alex side hugged Barrett.

"Greatest Best Man Ever." Holt grabbed Barrett and squeezed the life out of him.

"Thanks, guys." Barrett slapped Holt on the back before he released him. Grinning, he scurried to the get everything done. He wanted today to be perfect for his brother and best friend. Barrett met Holt when Frey saved him from bullies on their elementary school playground. Frey, Holt, and he became an inseparable trio from that day on, sharing every adventure. Alex joined sometimes, but since he was older, he made sure the trio stayed safe and out of trouble when their parents were working. With the DJ ready to start the entrance songs, Barrett strolled to the back to get the moms.

"Ladies, you both look beautiful." Barrett turned around and bent his elbows, waiting for Sehoy and Dyani to lock their arms with him. "Let's get this show started, shall we? Dyani, Alex will escort you in and mom, Holt's got you."

"Thank you, *chakpootsi*." Sehoy rubbed his forearm. "You look so handsome. One day, this will be you."

Barrett's step faltered. He was sure his mom noticed, but she kept the smile on her face and didn't say another word. He wished she wouldn't hold her breath waiting for his wedding, because it wasn't happening soon. Weddings and relationships were a lot of work, and he was enjoying his bachelorhood too much to be tied to one girl for the rest of his life.

"Ladies, you all look exquisite." Barrett told the bridesmaids as he passed them.

"Barrett, you're such a charmer." Maggie hip bumped him. Barrett chuckled, but didn't miss Mark's grimace as he pulled Maggie tighter to his side. Mark was overprotective. Barrett wished Mark luck taming that wild child. Maggie loved to bust Mark's balls and took every opportunity to do so. Misunderstandings were a bitch, and he was glad Mark held nothing against him after the one they'd had in Maggie's room with him naked in only a towel and Maggie in his shirt. *That had been a clusterfuck.*

"You look very handsome." Lizzy said when he reached her. She took his arm and caressed his bicep.

Fuck! "Thank you. You don't look too shabby yourself." Barrett had little practice turning down beautiful women, and Lizzy was beautiful—just not for him. To avoid another go-round with her, he stared ahead at the procession, silently enduring the tense quiet.

Gaby and Matteo led the way, followed by Maggie and Mark, Sarah and Grayhorse, Isa and Thunder, and then Lizzy and him. The boys went right, and the girls went left. After their crazy strip tease, they didn't have a rehearsal, so they did it this morning before the girls got ready. Barrett was grateful everyone knew where to go. Bryce and Tommy came next, each carrying a small pillow with a ribbon-tied bow holding their respective wedding rings. The boys stood in front of the groomsmen. Barrett put his hands on Bryce's shoulders to keep him steady. Tommy was old enough to manage without help.

Emmy followed Lucy down the aisle, throwing flower petals as they approached Alex and Holt. They looked so fucking adorable with their little lacey white puffy dresses. Emmy and Lucy stood in front of Sarah and Isa. Isa held Lucy's hand to keep her in place. Lucy looked up. Their eyes met and Barrett winked at her, a warm smile spreading across his face. Lucy beamed her lovely smile at him.

The opening chords of the bridal processional prompted all the guests to rise and face the back. The doors opened and Barrett sucked in his breath when he saw his twin with their dad, ready to walk down the aisle. Taking a quick glance at Holt, Barrett saw him grinning like a fool. *Shit, was he crying?* Barrett looked to Frey, and when she gazed at him, he lifted his chin toward Holt and smiled. *Frey winked at him. Fuck yeah, they were going to give Holt shit for crying at his wedding.*

After their dad handed Frey over to Holt and they stepped to the left of Uncle Spirit, Tori came down the aisle with Tall Bear. Tori was glowing as she walked to Alex. Her eyes were only for him. Barrett watched his brother beam at his bride. They stayed on the right side.

"Friends and family, today we will celebrate these two special unions with some of our traditions and some of yours." Uncle Spirit turned and grabbed two white blankets placed on a table behind him. Sehoy and Osceola took one to drape over Frey and Holt. Dyani and Tall Bear draped the other over Tori and Alex. Both sets of parents stepped back but stayed near them.

"These blankets are a part of our 'Blanket Ceremony'. We drape these blankets over the couple's shoulders to symbolize covering their sorrows and weaknesses. These blankets are special because their parents and grandparents used these same blankets." Uncle Spirit explained and then nodded to the parents. They took the blankets off their shoulders and held them on their laps, ready to pass them down.

"Next, we will do what is referred to as 'Smudging' in our culture." Uncle Spirit grabbed the smoking sage from the table and faced them. He moved his hand around the front of the couples. "Sage is used to cleanse a couple." When he finished, he cleansed himself and put the sage back on the table. "Now, onto the part of the ceremony you all know that needs no explanation from me."

Barrett, along with several guests, laughed.

"Gentlemen, I'm gonna start with you. Holt and Alex, will you take Frey and Tori, respectively, as your lawfully wedded wives? Will you honor and cherish them? Love, trust, and commit to them, through joy and pain, sickness and health, and whatever life may throw at you both, until death do you part?"

"I do." They each responded.

"Frey and Tori, do you accept Holt and Alex as your lawfully wedded husbands?" Will you honor and cherish them? Love, trust, and commit to them, through joy and pain, sickness and health, and whatever life may throw at you both, until death do you part?

"I do." They each responded.

"May I have the rings, please?" Uncle Spirit motioned to Bryce and Tommy.

"Bryce, follow Tommy." Barrett bent down and whispered in his ear.

Uncle Spirit waited for the boys to approach Holt and Alex. Then Holt and Alex pulled the rings off the pillows and thanked the boys.

"At this time, both Holt, Frey, Alex, and Tori will exchange rings. The wedding ring is a symbol of binding. A symbol of attachment and of belonging, not of possession, but of partnership. Tori and Alex wrote their own vows. Ladies first."

Tori and Alex faced each other. Tori slid Alex's ring on the tip of his finger.

"I promise that my love for you will be an ever-flowing spring, never diminished and always sweet and life-giving. You are my family, and I want to be there for you in all things. I am so excited to be your wife, and I vow to take from every moment the opportunity to love, nurture, and grow our family." Tori slid the ring in place when she finished.

Alex kissed her hand before he began his vows. "All I have in this world I will give to you. I promise to hold and keep you, comfort, protect, and shelter you for all the days of my life. I love the spark inside you, and I vow to help you release it into the world. Everyone should see the beautiful light inside you I see every day. You are the kindest, most sincere, loveliest woman I know. I feel blessed to walk beside you, be in your arms, and in your heart. Today, I affirm my love for you and can't wait to spend the rest of my life with you." Alex kissed her hand again after he slid her wedding band on his finger.

"Frey, your turn to go first." Uncle Spirit faced them.

Frey smiled at Holt and held his hand. "My commitment to you is one I give willingly, absolutely, and without hesitation. I have been yours since we were kids, and I saved you from bullies on the playground."

Holt nodded his head, agreeing with her. "You are right, my love."

"Happy Wife, Happy Life. It's good you've learned to agree with her." Barrett screamed out, heckling them and laughing with others.

"Shh." Frey pointed at Barrett before she turned back to Holt. "You are the love of my life and make me happier than I could have ever imagined. I feel blessed to be able to love you forever." Frey slid the ring on.

"Frey." Holt released a deep breath. "I promise to spend each day working on becoming the truest version of myself, for you, for us, and for our family. From this day forward, let us build a home together filled with love, laughter, joy, and light. I'm more than ready to build my life with you." Holt got choked up near the end of his vows. Barrett thought for sure he was going to cry again, but he held it in.

"Ladies, say your future husband's name and please repeat after me: Frey said Holt and Tori said Alex at the same time. I promise to love you and commit to you my whole life. I promise to be there for you when you need me, to be honest with you, to be faithful to you and you alone, and to walk through the valleys of life together, just as we will stand atop mountains together, too."

"Gentlemen, your turn. Say your future wife's name and please repeat after me: Holt said Frey and Alex said Tori at the same time. I promise to love you and commit to you my whole life. I promise to be there for you when you need me, to be honest with you, to be faithful to you and you alone, and to walk through the valleys of life together, just as we will stand atop mountains together, too."

"Stop!"

Chapter 13

Wedding Shitshow

BARRETT

Barrett turned his head and saw the beautiful blonde woman he'd first seen at the cultural center with a young child standing at the end of the aisle. Deputy Bryan was holding Sky back, probably because the woman wasn't armed just screaming like a crazy person. *What was she doing here?* Barrett watched her run up the aisle, followed by Deputy George.

"Please, stop the wedding. You all need to leave. There's trouble coming. Go! Get out!" The blonde woman stopped when she reached the wedding party.

Barrett stepped in front of her and grabbed her arms. She had a large bruise on her face, and sounded like a lunatic, and nothing was going to ruin his sister's day.

"Let me go." Pulling against Barrett, she cried out to get to the bride and groom. "Please listen to me."

"You!" Maggie screamed. "What the fuck are you doing here, bitch?"

Barrett turned his head just in time to see Maggie running towards them, her face flushed and her hair flying behind her. Maggie glared at the woman, her eyes narrowed and filled with icy fury. It looked like she was going to hit the blonde.

"Mark!" Barrett called out.

"I'm on it." Mark grabbed Maggie before she reached Barrett. "Come here, killer. Let's hear what she has to say before we throw punches."

"Miss Maggie, you owe me two dollars." Lucy interjected, picturing the money going into the swear jar.

"Shh, baby, not right now." Gaby moved toward Lucy and picked her up.

Barrett turned toward the blonde. "Let's start with your name, babe."

"Angel. My name's Angel." Angel grabbed Barrett's arms and shook him. "Please, you all must leave this place now. They're coming." Angel pleaded with Barrett.

"You get the fuck out!" Maggie screamed.

"Mark, she's not helping." Barrett hollered. "Why do we all have to leave? Who's coming?" Barrett bent down and shoved his face in front of her. "What the hell is going on?"

"Lucifer's Renegades are on their way and they're out for blood." Angel looked around at all the guests. "Hurry, get out!"

"How do you know this?" Barrett glared at Angel.

"Because I overheard their conversation and hurried over here to warn you as soon as I knew the location of the wedding. Please, you must listen to me." Angel's eyes watered.

Out of the corner of his eyes, Barrett noticed all the deputies surrounding the guests as they got up to exit down the aisle.

"Nobody is fucking up my brother and sister's weddings." Barrett screamed at Uncle Spirit. "Uncle Spirit, please finish the ceremony quickly."

Uncle spirit nodded and spoke the following words as quickly as possible.

"To my beautiful couples, having proclaimed your love and commitment to one another in the eyes of these loved ones, and with the power vested in me by *Wakan Tanka*, our Great Spirit, I am so happy to pronounce you *husband* and *wife*! You may kiss your brides!"

As soon as Uncle Spirit said his last word, gunshots rang out. An employee slumped against the far wall, then slowly fell to the floor as blood sprayed from a fatal gunshot wound to his head. Total pandemonium erupted as people screamed and raced for the exit. Barrett grabbed Angel and fell to his knees.

"Everybody, get down!" Deputy George shouted.

"I already called for backup." Deputy Bryan yelled at Deputy George. "I'm gonna head down with Sky. Keep everyone low."

Deputy George, Deputy Sean, and Holt guided all the guests to the farthest corner, away from the gunfire. Suddenly, they heard a loud roar, and one of the undercover deputies looked over the wall.

"Are more coming?" Barrett asked the nearest deputy, who had eyes on the commotion outside.

"It's Los Lobos and they're engaging with the LRs. Fuck, it's a bloodbath down there." The deputy's scream cut through the night as he stood watch.

Barrett knew he had to get out of there. He stood, bent at the waist, and pulled Angel's arm. "You're coming with me." Barrett dragged her toward the entrance to the hotel.

"José!" Maggie screeched and tried to run out the door. Barrett watched Mark tackle her and turn, so he took the brunt of their fall. He was trying to reason with her, but Barrett couldn't hear a word he was saying between the gunfire and screaming.

Barrett saw the men cover their women and children. Police sirens wailed from every direction around the resort and casino. The sound of several motorcycles speeding away, evading the police, faded into the distance.

Alex walked by him with Tori. "Follow me to the convention center kitchen. We can barricade in there until it's safe to come out."

Barrett and the guys helped guide everyone from the wedding into that room. It was going to be a tight fit, but under the circumstances, it was better than getting shot at.

Barrett stayed in the hallway guiding everyone, but he wasn't releasing Angel's hand, no matter how hard she tried to pull away.

"Barrett, let her go. We need to hide out." Lizzy tried to pull his arm away from Angel.

Motherfucker, he had to get Lizzy into the room and talk to Angel. He could only handle one irate girl at a time. Looking around, he spotted George inside the convention room, leading more people out. "George!" George turned to face him. "Please take Lizzy into the kitchen."

"Of course." George put his arm around Lizzy's waist and practically dragged her away from Barrett, kicking and screaming.

Fuckin' A, Lizzy needed to get over her crush on him, like yesterday.

"Let me go." Angel tugged and pulled. "They'll kill me if they find out I warned you."

"Who the hell are you?" Barrett stared at her.

"I'm Reaper's daughter." Angel was trembling and crying as she continued to struggle against Barrett's hold.

Shooting upright, Barrett pulled Angel close. "You're the daughter of the fucking president of Lucifer's Renegades? Why the fuck did you warn us?"

"Because." Angel's eyes showed the terror she felt inside. "I don't agree with all the shit they've done. And now they've turned my son against me. If they catch me, they'll treat me like a traitor and death will be better than what they will do to me. I need to grab my son and run. I told him to stay in the lobby and wait for me."

"Shit, there's a kid down there with the LRs." the shout came from a deputy standing by the wall.

"No, no!" Angel kicked Barrett in the shin and ran toward where the deputy was pointing.

A shot rang out, and Barrett saw the deputy duck for cover.

"Fuck! Angel! Get down!" A guttural roar ripped from Barrett's throat as the bullet ripped into his flesh—a blinding rage replaced the shock. "Motherfucker!" Barrett shoved Angel to the ground as the bullet's impact sent his body reeling backward, away from her, the sharp scent of gunpowder filling the air. Making a dangerous situation worse, he twisted his ankle when he stumbled over an upturned chair.

Angel took that moment to bolt toward the staircase.

"Fuck! Angel, get back here." Barrett bolted up, held his shoulder, which hurt like a bitch, and limped after her into the stairwell. "It's too dangerous for you down there." *Why wouldn't she fucking stop? He was trying to help her.* Maggie screamed, telling him to stop and get help. However, he was afraid to let Angel leave the hotel. He was sure the bullet that struck him was intended for her. Had he not pushed her head down, that bullet would've landed between her eyes, and she'd be dead. But, if she was Reaper's daughter, why the hell were they shooting at her?

Climbing the stairs hurt like a bitch with a sore ankle, but Barrett ignored the pain and continued down the flights of stairs until he caught up to her before she went out the front doors of the lobby. He saw a young boy riding bitch behind one biker as they drove off.

"Steele, no!" Angel screamed and would've collapsed to the ground had Barrett not wrapped his good arm around her from behind. "No! Let me go! That's my son! They have my son!" Angel's body shook uncontrollably as she reached her hands out as if to grab her son.

Barrett was not letting her go out there after they had already attempted to kill her once. With the gunshots ceased, police scrambled to apprehend as many members as they could from both clubs. It was a shitshow of epic proportions out there.

"Come on. I'm taking you to my room so we can talk." Barrett picked her up firefighter style and limped to the elevators.

"Are you crazy? I gotta go save my son, and you need medical attention. You're bleeding and you can barely walk." Angel slapped his ass. "Put me down!"

"I'm gonna drop your ass if you slap me again." Barrett growled at her. His shoulder was throbbing, and he could barely put weight on his ankle, but he had to get her out of harm's way. "I have a lot of questions, but first, I have to make sure my family is okay."

"No, first you gotta put me down. Then you need to see a doctor."

Barrett felt her hands lift his tux jacket. One hand slid down the small of his back into his pants before both hands grabbed onto his belt. *Fuck! What the hell was she doing back there? And why the hell was he turned on by this bossy ass woman?* This was not the time to think about sex. He'd just been shot. Unfortunately, his brain and his cock were not on the same wavelength. Having her breasts pressed against his back with her ass in his palms was short circuiting his brain and making his cock hard as a rock.

"Stop wiggling." Barrett slapped her ass as he stepped into the elevator.

"No," Angel glared at him through the mirrored walls. "I can walk, so put me down."

"Not a chance in hell." Barrett gritted his teeth, working through his pain. Glaring right back at her, he punched the button for his floor. Grateful for the quick ride up, he entered his room and dropped Angel on his bed. Locking the adjoining door to Alex's room and standing in front of his bedroom door so she couldn't make a run for it, he called Deputy George.

"George, is everyone alright?" Barrett watched Angel panting from exertion.

"Yeah, your family is good. It's lucky those gangs were so focused on each other, or who knows what could have happened to your family or the guests. Where are you? Are you okay? You don't sound too good." Deputy George rapid fired questions at Barrett.

"I need a doctor." Barrett leaned against the door. He was losing his adrenaline rush. "I took a bullet to my shoulder and fucked up my ankle."

"Are you fucking serious?" Deputy George yelled into the phone. "Where the fuck are you?"

"In my room, hurry." Barrett slid down the door and landed on his butt as Angel glared at him from the bed. "I have Angel."

"Who the fuck is Angel?" Barrett could hear Deputy George yelling at people to get a doctor and follow him.

"The blonde that interrupted the wedding." Barrett's words were slurring, and he kept blinking to stay awake. "George, please don't let my brother or sister know I was shot. I want them to go on their honeymoon tomorrow and at least enjoy that without worrying about me."

"I don't agree, but fine. I won't tell them tonight."

"Thanks, man." Barrett sighed. "I owe you one."

"Barrett!" Deputy George yelled. "Do not hang up! Stay with me on the phone."

Angel came over and took the phone from him. Barrett was in no condition to fight her.

"Whoever this is," –Angel spoke into the phone– "you need to hurry. He needs medical attention."

Angel placed the phone in Barrett's lap. "I'm sorry," she whispered and slowly opened the bedroom door, scooting Barrett aside.

"Please, stay with me," Barrett mumbled. Too weak to stop her from leaving. "Don't go out there. It's not safe."

"I have to get to my son." Angel squeezed through and left.

How could she leave him? Didn't she have a heart? He fucking took a bullet for her. With a sigh, Barrett hung his head, the bitter taste of betrayal filling his mouth as he realized a beautiful woman had played him. *I'm an idiot.*

Chapter 14

Arrests

MAGGIE

"Do you think they arrested José?" Maggie pulled Mark out of the kitchen by his tux's lapel. "Oh my God!" She stopped when Barrett ran by her with the blonde girl. "There's Barrett and I think he's bleeding. Where the hell is he going with that blonde bitch?"

"Killer, slow down." Mark grabbed her wrist and pulled her to the side of the hallway. "We are not following Barrett, and we are definitely not rushing down there to stop the police from arresting anyone. Do you want to wind up in jail for Obstruction of Justice?"

"Is that really a thing or did you just make it up, Surfer Smurf?" Maggie crossed her arms and stared him down.

"Preventing a police officer from performing their duties is one of the many reasons to be charged with Obstruction of Justice. I didn't make it up." Mark pivoted and pressed her up against the wall to keep her in place. "Since when are we back to Surfer Smurf instead of Big Sexy?" Mark quirked an eyebrow.

"Since you are blocking me from going to my brother. What if José's hurt?" Maggie pointed down the hallway. "What if he's down there right now calling out for me and I don't get to hear his last words?"

Mark knew Maggie would do anything to go downstairs and find her brother, but he also knew she'd witnessed her parents' deaths at the hands of Lucifer's Renegades. The thought of her going downstairs was unbearable, but what if she was correct, and José was hurt–or worse? He couldn't keep her from seeing her brother.

"Darlin'." Mark rested his forehead on hers and cupped her face. After a few deep breaths, he lifted her face up to his. "Come on. I'm gonna go with you. But if you run off on me, I'm gonna spank your ass so hard you won't be able to sit for a week. Do you hear me?"

"Yes, daddy." Maggie smirked.

Mark winced. "Do NOT call me daddy. You are not that much younger than me."

"Then stop ordering me around." Maggie shoved his chest with her arms.

"Let's just go," Mark grumbled. "We'll talk about this later, Trouble."

Maggie wrapped her arms around his neck and kissed him. "Thank you."

Mark grabbed her hand and Maggie heard him mumble. "I know I'm gonna regret this."

Downstairs, they saw police officers arresting several bikers, reading them their rights before putting them in the back of police cars. A cold sweat slicked Maggie's palms as she scanned the crowd, each unfamiliar face a potential threat. *Where was Barrett? Where was her brother?* Unfortunately, she came across some LRs who insulted her while the police were placing them in handcuffs. Mark steered her away from the group, the angry shouts fading as they distanced themselves, and the officers warned them to control their language.

"Over there." Mark pointed to another side of the parking lot where José was being arrested.

Maggie ran to him, screaming out his name.

"Can I have a minute, please?" José asked the arresting officer.

Maggie threw herself at him and hugged him. "I'm so glad you're okay. I was worried they killed you."

"Ma'am, I need to take him now." The officer grabbed José's arm.

"Please, my brother is a good man," Maggie pleaded with the officer. "He just makes bad choices sometimes."

"Clearly." The officer scoffed.

"Maggie, stop. It will be okay." José said while the officer dragged him away. "I'll call you as soon as I can. Mark, please, take care of my sister."

"You have my word." Mark nodded.

"Mark, help him." Maggie grabbed his bicep, attempting to pull him toward the police car with her brother now inside.

"Maggie, stop!" Mark's firm voice stopped Maggie in her tracks. He never called her Maggie unless he meant business. Usually, she was one of his silly names, like killer or darlin' if he was flirting with her, but never Maggie nor Margarita. Maggie's tears rolled down her face. *What if they hurt José in jail? Reaper was in jail. She wouldn't survive Reaper killing José.*

"Darlin'." Mark cupped her face, holding her gaze steady. "We'll get him an excellent lawyer and post bail as soon as we can." Mark pulled her into his arms. "Let's go upstairs. I don't like you being surrounded by the LRs even if most of them are being hauled off to jail."

Mark led her back inside to the room they were using on the family floor. *How had such a beautiful day turned into a horrible nightmare with her brother getting arrested and Barrett getting shot? Where was Barrett, anyway?* Maggie watched Mark make a few phone calls before she went into the bathroom, washed off her makeup, changed her clothes, and climbed into bed.

"I've arranged for a lawyer to go speak with your brother immediately." Mark said as he took off his tuxedo.

"Have you called Barrett? Is he okay?" Maggie could see Mark out of the corner of her eye, but she was so tired, she just wanted to sleep and wake up tomorrow to a different dream.

"I tried. He's not answering his phone." Mark hung up the tux and headed to the bathroom.

"Can you please try again?" Maggie yawned. She was crashing fast, but she didn't want to go to sleep until she found out that Barrett was okay. Maggie could hear Mark talking, but wasn't sure who was on the other line.

Mark came out of the bathroom. "Barrett got a bullet in the shoulder, but it went all the way through. A medic is patching him up. He's going to be okay. He just needs to rest." Mark spooned her and held her tight. "Hell, we all need to rest after this crazy night."

Maggie scooted back into his body and sighed. "I'll check on Barrett tomorrow. I just hope José will be okay in jail tonight."

"It's gonna be okay." Mark kissed her cheek. "We'll help your brother any way we can."

Chapter 15

The Day After

MARK

Mark didn't sleep well last night. He couldn't stop tossing and turning, trying to figure out how to help José. But until he talked to him, Mark wasn't sure how he could help. *Had José killed someone? Was it self-defense?* By the time he and Maggie found José, the fighting and shooting had ended. He didn't see any marks on José's body from a fight. But he also couldn't see José's knuckles because the officer had already cuffed him.

Hopefully, the high-priced lawyer he put on retainer for José would get him some answers. He was expecting a phone call this morning. Maggie had also been restless last night, and no amount of loving had calmed her down enough to sleep. Between the two of them, they were lucky to get over four hours of sleep.

Maggie rolled over and laid her hand on his chest. Mark slipped his arm under her and rubbed her back.

"Good morning," Maggie mumbled.

"Mornin' Darlin.'" Mark kissed her forehead. "I'd ask you how you slept, but between both of us tossing and turning, I'm pretty sure we both slept like shit."

"Yeah. Every time I stopped thinking about José in prison with Reaper, I thought about Barrett getting shot. I want to check on both today. I know my brother has done some horrible things, but I thought he was doing better." Maggie ran her hands over his chest.

"Darlin', he's committed murder before. You know he should be in prison, right?" Mark wasn't trying to be mean, but her brother had committed three murders following their parents' deaths. In the eyes of the law, it doesn't matter if it was an eye for an eye—murder was a felony. Mark knew he couldn't keep José out of jail, but if he could make things easier for Maggie, then he would do what he could.

Watching their interaction yesterday during his arrest, José seemed calm and complacent. He looked like a man ready to pay the piper for his deeds. Mark just wondered how he would do in jail with some of Lucifer's Renegades members, especially Reaper. During the search for José, he saw many Los Lobos members arrested. At least José would have some of his brothers with him. The question now was whether or not he would be granted bail. If they convicted and imprisoned José, Mark hoped they would send him to a nearby facility so Maggie could visit whenever she wanted. It was just too early to know what would happen next.

"I know." Maggie sighed. "I've always known he would end up dead or in jail. He would probably prefer to be dead, but I can't lose my brother, too. Is that selfish of me?"

Mark rolled them over and leaned on his elbows, gazing into her eyes. He would do anything to ease her worry and put a smile on her face. But his Maggie was brave and resilient. She could overcome any challenge, one day at a time. With his fingers burrowed in her hair, he poured all his love into their morning kiss.

"No, darlin'. You love your brother, and you remember all the good times growing up. He's made his choices, but he's always loved you and tried to protect you as best as he could. There is nothing wrong with wishing he's alive and still in your life." Mark cupped her face with one hand, stroking her cheek with his thumb. "I promise you, if he gets sentenced to a prison term, I will take you to see him as often as you want. You will not lose your brother."

"Thank you." Maggie raised her hand and laid it against his cheek.

Mark removed her hand from his cheek and held it between them, running his thumb over her engagement ring. "This ring means I will commit to you and stand beside you for the rest of our lives. We are together forever and into the afterlife. I love you, your family, your friends, and I will love our future six children."

"Six children!" Maggie's eyes bugged out.

Mark wanted to lighten the mood, so he threw out the first number that popped in his head. He'd always wanted a big family, but six sounded excessive. Especially since the world caters to a family of four or less. When he was younger growing up in Montana, where ranchers have lots of kids to help with the ranch work, their family of four always got seated faster at restaurants and hotels were easier to book because you didn't need a suite.

Mark loved kids and would take as many as Maggie wanted to give him. Hell, if they couldn't have kids, he would gladly adopt. Watching Frey and Holt going through the adoption process for Bryce was inspiring. Bringing a child into their family would be a wonderful gift for any of the other shelter boys.

"Too many?" Mark quirked his eyebrow. "How about two and we practice a lot?"

"I can get on board with that." Maggie pushed her pelvis into him. "We can even adopt a shelter boy. I love those kids."

"You read my mind, darlin'." Mark took her hand and placed it over his shoulder. Leaning down, he traced his tongue over her bottom lip before opening his mouth for a kiss that was full of promise and love. He would never get enough of her. Her taste, her smell, the feel of her soft breasts pressed against his hard chest. Everything about Maggie consumed his thought and feelings.

Mark stroked her nipple while his tongue trapped hers and sucked it into his mouth. Maggie ran her hand down his back and grabbed his ass, pulling him toward her. She couldn't move him, but he got the hint and laid on top of her, giving her what she was asking for. He would always give her what she wanted, especially in bed. Maggie spread her legs and reached for his cock, placing it at her entrance.

Mark released her mouth, licking and sucking his way down to her breasts.

"I need you." Maggie gyrated her hips up to his, coating his cock with her juices.

Mark sucked her breast and twirled his tongue around her nipple, savoring the perking bud before he raised his head and stared into her eyes. In one swift move, he thrust into her, sinking all the way down. He desired to watch her come completely undone, just like he did every time he entered her body – she consumed his heart and soul.

Maggie wrapped her arms and legs around him. Reaching behind Maggie, he cupped her ass and tilted it so he could slide even deeper. Mark didn't want any space between them as he slowly made love to his girl.

"I love you." Mark groaned.

Maggie's moans got louder, and she closed her eyes.

"Open your eyes, darlin'. I want to see your ecstasy...," Mark's thrusts became harder and faster after every point he was making, "your arousal...your release... and your love...in those beautiful eyes."

Maggie's eyes blinked and opened for him.

"I love you too. With all my heart." Maggie whispered.

Mark's heart pounded in his chest to a frantic drumbeat as Maggie's muscles tightened around his cock before the intensity of her orgasm washed over him in a wave of electric heat. Mark always used protection, but this time, he wanted to feel her surrounding him. After all, Mark was eager to marry Maggie and start a family. If Maggie wasn't ready to be a mother, they needed to talk about other birth control options because from now on, he wanted to be inside her with no barriers.

Not wanting to crush Maggie, Mark rolled them over and Maggie sprawled out on top of him. They remained connected, neither one wanting to release the other. Mark ran one hand through her hair while the other massaged her back.

The insistent ringing of his phone sliced through the quiet, causing him to reach for it on his nightstand.

"Mr. Stone." It was the lawyer he got José. It was about time he called. "What's going on?"

"I'm here with José. He wants to talk to his sister."

"Darlin', Mr. Stone is the lawyer I hired for José." Mark put the phone on speaker and handed it to Maggie.

"José?" Maggie scrambled to sit up while holding the phone.

"*Hermanita. ¿Cómo estás?*"

"I'm fine, but how are you? José, what's happening?" Maggie's eyes bouncing between the phone and Mark.

"I'm good. We're trying to make a deal with the DA. We're calling from my lawyer's phone because jail phones record conversations and our deal is confidential."

"What do you have to do?" Maggie squinted at the phone.

"Not sure yet, but I need Mark to post bail. I just had my first appearance with the judge and bail is set at $20,000 because I'm not a flight risk."

"I will head down there within the next hour and pay it." Mark swung his legs to the side of the bed.

"Do you need a place to stay? Should you stay away from the clubhouse?" Maggie got out of bed on her side.

"I'm not sure yet. I'll know more after you post bail. Can you come get me? My bike is still at the resort unless they towed it."

"Yes, I'll be there in twenty." Mark hollered on his way to the bathroom. He didn't have to scream so loud because Maggie had grabbed the phone and was right behind him. "We'll look in the parking lot for your bike before we leave. Have Mr. Stone text me a description of the bike and the tag number."

"If it's here, I can drive it to you," Maggie blurted.

"No. Absolutely not." Mark started the shower and stared her down. "I will drive it to him."

"He's let me drive his bike before." Maggie huffed.

"I'm sure he has, but if any LRs are on the lookout for his bike, I'd rather they see me and not you driving it." Mark raised his eyebrow as he attempted to make his point and have her not argue with him.

"Mark's right." José's voice ended that argument. "The LRs know the bike I ride, and I'm sure they've memorized my plate number. Please do what he says, *hermanita*. I'll get one of my brothers to get my bike."

"Fine." Maggie stomped her foot.

Mark was glad José was on his side. An angry Maggie was hard to sway.

"Okay." Mr. Stone came back on the line. "I will text you his info. Text me after you post bail."

Chapter 16

New Year's Day - Happily Ever After...Finally

Frey

Weddings were supposed to be beautiful joyous occasions, but theirs had turned into a war zone between two rival biker gangs trying to kill each other, as well as Tori and Maggie. *What a fucking shitshow?* They didn't even get to have a normal reception with the fireworks they planned at midnight. The only fireworks they experienced was gunfire.

At least the food was neatly packaged in Styrofoam containers. Her parents gathered as many guests as possible and gave them a to-go reception dinner. The leftover food became a special menu item at Savor. Who wouldn't want a discounted filet or lobster dinner?

Damn biker gangs had ruined their beautiful moment. Frey hoped it wasn't a prelude to a shitty year. Maybe they could have a one-year celebration reception or a party when they got back from their two-week honeymoon in Hawaii – a gracious gift from family and friends for both couples. It would be fun to do some things with her bestie and brother.Although Frey was most excited about spending time with Holt in their private bungalow.

For once, Frey jumped out of bed before Holt and took her quickest shower ever. After last night, she was ready to get out of town.

"Get up sleepy head," Frey hollered at Holt on her way into the closet. Just as she finished packing her clothes, she heard the shower stop. Wanting to take care of her man, she strolled into the bathroom to have his towel ready for him.

Holt pushed the curtain open and took his towel. "Well, you look ready to go."

"After last night, I'm ready to blow this popsicle stand." Frey stared at his cock and licked her lips. Several drops of water ran down his beautifully sculpted chest down to the tip while he dried his head and shoulders.

"Hey, eyes up here." Holt pointed to his face. "Do not mention a popsicle, stare at my cock, and lick you lips in the same breath. We don't have time. We gotta meet Tori and Alex in the lobby to catch our ride to the airport."

"I know, but he's so yummy." Frey glanced down and saw 'he' was now standing at attention.

"Well, 'he,'" –Holt wrapped the towel around his waist and made air quotes when he said 'he'– "will have to wait until we get to Hawaii because I don't want to miss our flight. Behave and stop tempting him."

Frey laughed because their conversation got crazier by the minute. As if Holt's cock had a mind of his own. And maybe he did because the tent in his towel was not dropping.

"I can help you with that." Frey pointed at it.

"I'm fine," Holt growled. "Don't you have to finish packing?" Holt brushed his teeth.

"I'm done packing my stuff and you look like you're in pain." Frey stared at his cock through the mirror. "I can be quick."

Holt spit out the paste in his mouth,rinsed, and spit out again. "Seriously? You're not helping." Holt put all his toiletries in a pouch and left it on the counter.

Holt whipped the towel off and hung it up.Frey followed him out of the bathroom and pushed him to the bed. Holt turned,sitting on his ass. "Frey, we don't have time."

"We always have time." Frey pushed him back and slid to her knees, wrapping her mouth around his cock. Frey heard Holt groan and felt his hands in her hair. She knew once his sexy cock entered her mouth, he would be putty in her hands, and she would be in control of his orgasm.

Holt exploded in her mouth and relaxed on the bed. "Thank you. I'll take care of you when we get there. I'm sure I'll be hungry. I love you."

"Love you too. Now get up or we're gonna be late." Frey slapped his abs, and his body curled up.

"So, it's my fault now?" Holt chuckled.

"Yep, didn't you hear my brother yesterday say, 'Happy Wife, Happy Life'?" Frey grabbed his duffle and put it on the bed,ready to fill it with his clothes.

"Yeah." Holt stood and headed to the closet. "But I don't think that means you're never at fault."

"Uh, in my book, it does. Once you realize I'm always right, I'll be happy, and you'll have a good life," Frey rambled while she threw his underwear and bathing suits in the duffle. She'd let him pick out his other clothes since they were in the closet.

"I see how it is." Holt chuckled and walked out of the closet dressed, carrying his clothes that needed to go into the duffle. "Can you grab my flip-flops?"

Frey threw them at his feet. "If we forgot anything, we'll get it there." Frey went to grab her rolling bag.

"Step aside, woman." Holt grabbed her hips and pushed her away from her bag. "My bride is not carrying luggage, if I can help it." Holt kissed her. "See, I can make you happy."

"You sure can, my big, strong, sexy man." Frey winked at him.

Holt grinned and placed his duffle on top of her rolling bag. "Grab anything else you need and let's go."

"Yes, sir."

"I'm gonna fuck that sassiness out of you as soon as we reach our honeymoon suite." Holt said on his way past her. Then held their room door open for her to walk through on her way to the elevator.

"Promises, promises, big boy," Frey said over her shoulder.

"One I plan to fulfill to the best of my ability tonight."

Frey couldn't wait.

*** Tori ***

"Do we have everything?" Tori was running around the bedroom, opening and closing drawers frantically, making sure she packed everything she needed.

"Baby." Alex wrapped his arms around her from behind and rested his chin on her shoulder. "If we forget anything, I'llbuy it when we get there. Relax. Everything's going to be okay."

"I just don't want to spend any money on something I could've brought from home." As a member of the Oglala Lakota Tribe, Tori grew up on the Pine Ridge Reservation in South Dakota which is considered the poorest Native American tribe in the United States due to the high unemployment rate and a large percentage of the population living below the poverty line. Her parents taught her to make do with what she had and only purchase items that were necessities, not luxuries.

Alex's tribe was wealthier than hers since they owned several casinos, but she didn't want Alex to think she was a gold digger. She loved Alex for who he was, not his bank account. Not that Alex was rich, but he got paid well as a chef and could save money since he lived at the resort and didn't have to pay for rent or food. Still, she didn't want to spend his money needlessly.

Alex turned her to face him.

"I love that about you." Alex cupped her face and kissed her. "But we need to get going. I'm sure Frey and Holt are already downstairs."

"Okay." Tori sighed.

"I'll grab the bags, if you'll get the door." Alex pushed their rollaway bags.

Tori had only flown once before to Florida from the reservation. Scared of losing their luggage, she made Alex pack their clothes in separate, smaller bags for the overhead bins. Their destination was warm, so packing was easy with just swimsuits, t-shirts,shorts, and dresses.

When they reached the lobby, Frey and Holt were standing with Sehoy, Osceola, Dyani, and Tall Bear, waiting for them.

Frey ran to Tori when she saw her wrapping her up in a tight embrace.

"Oh my God, this is so exciting!" Frey jumped up and down, while Tori remained still. "Why aren't you as excited as me?" Frey stopped and stared at her like she had grown an extra head overnight.

"I'm just afraid I forgot something." Tori bit her lip.

"We'll buy it there if we forgot it." Frey told her.

"I already told her that, but my wife is frugal with our money." Alex kissed her cheek. "Which I love about her, but now I want her to relax and enjoy our honeymoon." Alex left them and pushed their luggage to Holt and Sehoy.

"Alex is right." Frey grabbed her arm and wrapped it around hers. "We're going to fucking Hawaii for two weeks with our sexy hubbies."

Frey pulled her and started skipping toward the boys. Frey's excitement was contagious and before she knew it, Tori was smiling and skipping along beside her.

"Ladies, are you ready to go?" Osceolagave Tori a hug. "We will drive you guys to the airport in our resort van."

"Thank you so much." Tori released him to finish hugging Sehoy and her parents.

"Wait." Frey spun around. "Where's Barrett?"

"Uh," Osceola glanced at Sehoy, "he must have slept in."

"We were talking last night." Sehoy motioned her hands, including all the parents. "Since you didn't have a proper reception, we would like to have a party for you guys when you get back. We'll shoot off the fireworks then."

"That is very sweet of you." Tori was the first to speak. "But I don't think my parents can afford to come down again."

"We will pay for their tickets." Osceola nodded. "Do not worry."

"And we will still do a small celebration for you both the next time you come to visit us," Tall Bear spoke up. "I know our tribal council will want to celebrate your marriage. Just let us know when you can come, and your mom and I will set everything up."

"Really?" Tori smiled at her father.

"Yes." Tall Bear nodded. "Osceola, you and your family are welcome to join us."

"We would love that." Osceola wrapped his arm around his wife.

"Okay, that's settled then. Let's get you kids to the airport." Sehoy ran ahead of them, out the front doors. Tori saw her waving her arms and looking from left to right. *Who was she waving to?* The Rock 'n' Roll Resort & Casino's van was already parked in front, its side doors open. Suddenly, all their parents ran outside and as she approached the doors with Alex, she noticed some of her friends and guests lined up on either side of the doorway.

She hoped they would not throw rice or birdseed. The tradition of throwing rice was a time-honored practice that symbolized fertility, prosperity, and good luck for the newlywed couple. But she'd read somewhere that rice could harm the environment and the bird population by expanding in their stomachs. Bird seed was equally detrimental because if it was old or rotten, it could make birds sick and if it was wet and clumped together, it caused problems for the birds that tried to eat it.

As soon as Frey walked out, Tori saw they were blowing bubbles instead of rice or birdseed. She should've known her family would never do anything to harm nature or the animals that lived in it.Tori relaxed and walked out after Holt with Alex behind her. They were all saying goodbye to everyone before they got in the van heading to the airport.

"I can't believe Barrett missed this?"Alex grumbled. "It's not like him."

"It's not like him to miss saying goodbye." Holt wrapped his arm around Frey.

"I'm gonna kill him if he got drunk and is hungover." Frey crossed her arms.

"Maybe he didn't hear his alarm?" Tori scooted next to Alex and rubbed his thigh. Everyone was getting angry at Barrett, and she wanted to calm them down.

"I don't think so." Alex shook his head."I'm gonna call him."

"Hello?" Everyone heard Barrett's morning voice because Alex put him on speakerphone.

"Where the hell are you?" Alex yelled.

"Yeah, our Best Man is turning into our Worst Man," Holt interjected.

"Sorry." Barrett coughed, but Tori thought it sounded forced. "I don't feel well. But I hope you all have a great time on your honeymoon."

"Loser." Frey screamed into the phone. "You should've come down to see us off, then gone back to bed."

"I know. I'll make it up to you guys when you get back."

"How the hell are you going to do that?" Alex quirked an eyebrow and looked at everyone.

"I'll pick you all up from the airport when you get back and take you to a nice dinner. How about that?"

"Deal." Frey nodded.

"Done." Alex agreed.

"Okay. Well, you all have fun in the sun,and I'll see you in a couple of weeks."

"Bye, Barrett." Tori leaned down toward the phone. "Thank you for everything you did for us on our wedding."

"Even if it turned into a shitshow," Alex mumbled.

"Yeah, Best Man Ever!" Holt held his fist up, even though Barrett couldn't see him.

"Yeah, yeah, yeah. I gotta go."

They all said goodbye and talked about all the places they wanted to go to in Hawaii and things they wanted to do.

Chapter 17

Special Thanks

NERI

Thank you to my wonderful friend Michelle, who brainstorms with me as I write these stories. Your input is invaluable to me.

To all of my officer friends—Thank you, Thank you, Thank you! You all are making a difference in protecting us every day, and I am so very grateful for all you do. Please stay safe out there.

I needed to find a new book editor who could meet my tight deadlines. My exceptional friend, Deb Krickovich, stepped up to the plate and will be my new editor. Deb, I can't thank you enough for your help and advice.

I would like to give a special thanks to my readers. I am grateful for your ongoing support.

Chapter 18

About the Author

Neri Lopez

Neri Lopez has worn many hats as a stay-at-home mom of triplets, graphic designer, and high school teacher (Spanish, Art, and Graphic Design). She lives in Florida with her husband, grown kids, and their fur babies, Mocha and Chewy. She is a crafter of all trades, including crocheting (several craft shows a year), jewelry making, scrapbooking, knitting, sewing, and painting.

Neri loves to hear from her readers, contact her at:
website: sirenbookandcraft.com
(When you sign up for her newsletter, you will receive a FREE downloadable bookmark of Red Path.)

Please consider writing a review on Amazon and/or Goodreads after you read Neri's books. It helps her books be more visible on Amazon.

Or follow her on:
facebook: Neri Lopez - Author
instagram: Neri_Lopez_Author
(She is most active on facebook)

The Path Series
Book 1: Red Path (available on Amazon)
Book 2: Unconquered Path (available on Amazon)
Book 3: Wagering Path (available on Amazon)
Book 4: Unexpected Path (available on Amazon)
Novella Book 4.5: Double Trouble Path (available on Amazon)
Book 5: Twisted Path (2025)
Book 6: Blue Path (2025)